MURDER AMONG THE ROSES

BETH BYERS

CHAPTER 1

"*A*re you worried?" Violet sniffed, dabbing her nose with a handkerchief, and scowled at the grey drizzle outside the window. She had become well and truly drenched on the way to the train even with her thick coat. Her shoes were wet, her stockings were damp, and she wanted to curl up into a bed, near a fire, with a hot toddy or tea or coffee. Anything that was hot. At that moment, even hot water would be delightful.

"Ah…whyever would I be worried?" Victor cleared his throat and attempted an idle glance out the window as though Violet didn't know him too well for that nonsense. Even without the ending squeak to his question, she'd never have believed his playacting.

Violet laid her head on Victor's shoulder, patting his hand mockingly. On his other side, their friend Kate squeezed his free hand with more sympathy. She was, after all, much kinder than Vi.

Violet's attention was caught by the scene outside. Not so much the buildings but the grey skies and the way the rain beat against the glass. She was certainly home, she thought. The clatter and rocking of the train was possibly one of the strongest signs that they'd returned from their vacation. The steamship had been fun. Violet had danced every night with her beau, Jack. She had been kissed under the stars.

The visit to Cuba had been sun, sand, and too much rum. Her favorite memory was being alone at the ocean with Jack, feet in the waves, rum cocktail in hand.

Coming home, however, was an unwelcome awakening. After adjusting to Cuba, Violet felt as though she'd gone to the Antarctic in coming home. When you added in that Jack had been called into a case and disappeared into suspects, evidence, and interviews, Violet well and truly objected.

She had thought to distract herself with shopping with Lila and Gwen. Only, Gwen had been beckoned home because she'd been 'flitting about' to an 'unhealthy' extent. Whereas Lila and Denny had been drawn back to the Lake Country for something about the wild little sister. Violet pushed away those thoughts and returned to the restless movement of her twin.

"Perhaps you would be worried," Violet suggested lightly, "given you spent a significant pile of blunt on a house—sight unseen. There should certainly be a pause due to buying the furnishings, paper, and carpets in a whirlwind shopping trip without nearly enough deliberation? Or, perhaps you recall the bumbling reaction of the poor clerk you dumped the problem on?"

Victor muttered, "I'm sure he's a capable enough fellow. The letters were...ah...well...informative." Victor sounded sick.

He shifted, unsettling Violet's head on his shoulder, crossed his legs, and then uncrossed them. Violet's laugh had her twin jiggling his knees. He cleared his throat, choked a little, and then tried to clear his throat again.

"You're about to visit a house you purchased while you were drunk. You've never even seen this place. It could be anything." Violet might love laying those facts out too much. She just found the way he squirmed so very rewarding.

"Ah..." Victor cleared his throat yet again. "Ah..."

"You're a grandiloquent lad, aren't you?" Kate sniffed and then leaned forward to wink at Violet. The two of them smirked at each other and then in near-synchronization turned and grinned at Victor.

Victor groaned and told Kate, "You're supposed to be on my side. I feel sure that is how things should be."

Kate chuckled and leaned back again. "It'll be all right, boy-o. Things have a way of working out. If nothing else, perhaps you can find some other gin-sodden lad to shuffle the house off onto."

Victor snorted. "I think I might have been the only one foolish enough for that trick."

Kate squeezed his hand. "Between us, we'll work it out." A moment later she added, "I have a fierce craving for one of those rum cocktails you made. I'm so glad you bought so much rum."

Violet could go for a warm rum. She wasn't sure she'd like it, but it might cause this ceaseless shivering to finally give up the ghost. Even cold, Violet knew Kate had changed the subject to give Victor breathing space about his possibly massive mistake.

"I've got a man who'll send me more as well," Victor said. "Sweet Javier, the brilliant bartender in Havana, was a brother of my heart. Our souls aligned. I will miss him fiercely, desperately even."

"You did seem to fall deeply in love with him," Violet said. "I did as well. If not for Jack, I might have thrown myself into Javier's arms and begged him to love me forever."

"I am pretty sure," Kate said dryly, "that he already had several girl-friends. You'd have to join the queue."

"He was a genius with a cocktail shaker and had the most lovely eyes. Who wouldn't love him?" Violet laughed, then observed, "This house is very much in the country."

"More than I had thought," Victor said, sounding displeased. "What have I done?"

"That is the mystery, isn't it?" Kate adjusted her book on her lap. "When I told my mother I was coming with you to see the house you'd bought..."

"Did you tell her the whole story?"

"I sure did, boy-o." Kate shivered and tucked her coat closer.

Violet shivered herself, the sight of Kate's chill reminding Violet that she was wet too. She sniffed and dabbed her nose.

Victor groaned. "She barely likes me as it is. She sent me quite the scolding letter after your father received our gift."

"*Your* gift—I told you not to do it. Mama already thinks Papa drinks too much. You gave him a full case of rum, Victor. After meeting Mama, you should have known better."

"Don't forget the cigars," Violet laughed and then coughed on her laugh. The shivers were increasing in intensity despite the body heat of the nearly full train. The low level chatter of the fellow passengers was irritating her far more than usual. She tried to ignore the noise but she wasn't able to shake it off.

Victor whimpered at the thought of Mrs. Lancaster and lit a cigarette, trying and failing to pretend that he was unbothered. Neither Kate nor Violet were taken in.

Kate nodded seriously. "I told you not to do it."

"They're so good," Victor whined. "Maybe the best I've ever had. Your father likes them. He sent me quite the effusively grateful note."

"Yet, my mother will never forget. You'll hear about it every time you see her from now on. Could Papa's gratitude be worth Mama's grudge?"

Violet turned to hide her grin. There was an understanding between those two even if they hadn't put words to the feeling—not to her, not to each other, maybe not even to themselves. Violet couldn't be happier about Victor's choice. She had always been half-afraid Victor would fall for some vain idiot who only thought about money and clothes.

Violet smirked. She thought rather a lot about money and clothes, but she hoped there was more substance to her than that. Kate, on the other hand, had more substance than both Victor and Violet combined. She was kind, generous of action and thought. She read Shakespeare as though they were bedtime stories. She had even decided to learn Greek in Cuba. While the twins had bought clothes, rum, and cigars, Kate had purchased books to sharpen her already existing Spanish skills, and even found some English-to-Greek books for her new language pursuit.

Violet had danced on the beach and Kate had observed the difference in the wildlife on a Cuban beach compared to British beaches. Victor, on the other hand, had walked beside her, drink in hand, listening to her and deciding they needed to visit more beaches so she could continue her observations. Violet hadn't missed the way that Kate's eyes had brightened at the idea.

Violet fell asleep on Victor's shoulder while Kate read the remainder of the ride. When the train stopped, Violet jerked awake. She shivered, sneezed, and then looked up in horror at Victor. "Oh, no."

"Oh, Vi," he said, handing her his handkerchief. Her lace piece of nothing wasn't going to be enough.

She sneezed in reply, once, twice, and a third time and then moaned, "I want a bed."

"I'll get you there, darling." He took her bag and Kate's as well, leading the way. On the way to exit the train, Violet shivered and leaned into Kate for warmth.

"Kate," Violet said after another sneeze. "I'm terrible at being ill. I'll apologize now and then again when I'm better. I may disappear entirely. Should Victor get ill—" Violet glanced at Victor, winked, and told Kate, "Flee, flee at once."

"Darling," Victor said, glancing back and winking himself. "Don't tell such terrible tales."

Violet scowled at her brother as he handed her down from the train. She didn't even wait for Kate, just left them both, heading immediately into the train station to avoid a further chill. It was too late. She tried pulling her coat tighter, but it was still damp.

"Hurry, Victor," Violet muttered, knowing he was arranging their luggage and finding their transportation.

"There, there, love," Kate said when she joined Vi a moment later. Kate tugged Violet to nearby seats and then pressed Vi's head down onto her shoulder.

Violet snuggled in, whimpering a little.

"All will be well. We'll get into the auto, get you to the house, light a fire, and get you a big cup of tea or broth."

"Oh, hello there," someone said as Violet sneezed. "Oh, dear me. Ill, are you?"

"We got a bit of a chill and sat damp on the train," Kate said. "We'll get her warmed up and all will be well."

"Not with that red nose," the person said. "You're in for it, love."

Violet pushed upright, eyeing the woman who didn't hesitate at bad news. She was middle-aged with a little grey in her hair, and blue-eyed behind her small spectacles. Her expression was friendly enough, but the tight collar, smooth bun, and long wool skirt made Violet wonder if the woman hadn't realized rising hems were all the rage.

The woman smiled and set aside a basket with knitting needles sticking out of it. "Are you visiting?"

"My brother bought a house here," Violet said, sniffing and dabbing her nose with a handkerchief.

"The old Higgins place?"

"Ah, perhaps?"

"Is your brother the drunk London man who bought the house in a bar?"

Violet's lips twitched and she nodded.

"Interesting." The woman's lips twitched in reply, her eyes bright with interest and humor, and Violet winked at her before she sneezed again.

Then Vi moaned a little and muttered, "I hope Victor has things sorted out."

"I'm Agnes King," the woman said, holding out her hand.

Violet shook it, as did Kate who introduced them. "This is Lady Violet Carlyle. I am Kate Lancaster. We've come to see what Mr. Carlyle has done."

Mrs. King lifted a brow. "I'd have thought you'd be here before now, to be honest. We've had a bit of a wager going on when he would show up or if he would. I've lost by six weeks."

Violet laughed and Kate smirked.

"I believe my brother was in a bit of denial." The shivers were becoming more intense, as was her headache. Pressure was mounting behind Violet's forehead, and she'd have whined if not for Agnes King.

Violet didn't get sick very often, but when she did, she tended to go down fast and hard. Violet sniffed once again, trying to delicately hide the fact that snot was starting to pour from her nose.

"Well," Mrs. King said, "that seems about the right reaction for someone who bought a house sight unseen."

"Is it a terrible house?" Kate asked, clearly hoping it wasn't too awful.

Mrs. King shook her head. "It's nice enough. It needed work. We've seen the carpenters and the like come and go. I imagine it's a snug little place now. Certainly with semi-competent fellows hired. It was always a snug place, astounding gardens, quite a nice ballroom, and library. I believe it was sold with the furniture and contents. Perhaps you'll find some treasure."

"Wouldn't that be fun?" Kate said when Violet dabbed her nose in answer. "Something to tell our friends when we go home."

"Do you not intend to live here?" The voice snapped a bit with anger. Violet caught the feeling that Mrs. King seemed to be willing to welcome them until just that moment.

Oh-oh, Violet thought, Mrs. King didn't seem happy at that idea.

"Not full-time," Violet admitted. "Our lives are in London."

"I suppose you are nightclub-going, cocktail-drinking, jazz music-listening, bright young things? Full of vigor and fun and very little responsibility? The garden deserves to be protected and kept up. Our little village deserves denizens who help improve the tenor of our life here."

Violet blinked as she digested that thinly-veiled diatribe. She wouldn't say that they were quite so frivolous. Yes to all the things that Mrs. King listed, but not entirely without something more to them. As for the garden, Violet was sure that Victor had said something about the gardener being the one who had been looking after the house in between the workers coming and going.

"We do enjoy those things," Violet said, "along with many other things. I understand the rose gardens here are quite remarkable?"

"I fear you'll find very little that you're used to in London here among our humble people," Mrs. King stated. "We do, however, have quite lovely gardens about."

Kate said dryly, "We don't expect to find the charms of London in the countryside. We've come for the charms of the country. I've read a little travel journal about this part of the country and have a list of things to see before we finish this visit. Violet and Victor are determined to go bicycling and horseback riding. I'd like to do nothing more than find a good spot for a picnic and to read a book in the grass. Do you have any recommendations of places we might visit?"

CHAPTER 2

*I*t took Victor far longer than expected to appear in the train station with rescue at hand. When he finally did appear, he was scowling. The look of tight anger on his face had Vi lifting her brows.

"The gardener was supposed to take an auto for us and be here. He only *just* arrived. In the meantime, Giles and I hired someone to take the things we brought for the house. They've left with our luggage, Beatrice, and the dogs, so Beatrice will be ready to coddle you the moment you've arrived. Ah…" He just realized they'd been speaking with Mrs. King and smiled winningly at her. "Hullo, there. I fear I'm a bit grumpy. I didn't see you at all."

"To be understood," Mrs. King said. "No matter. Traveling does push one's patience. It doesn't help when Philip Jones was neglectful once again."

"May I present Mrs. Agnes King?" Kate said. "We've just been making friends and inquiring after good picnic spots."

"You do look so much like your sister," Mrs. King said. "It's rather shocking."

Victor winked at Violet, who sneezed and told Mrs. King, "I had the good fortune to be a twin."

The twins were opposite sides of the same coin. They were both tall and slim with dark hair and eyes. They each had sharp features and pale skin, though Victor had tanned quite a bit in Cuba. Violet, on the other hand, had safeguarded her complexion with large hats.

"Did you find good places to picnic? I am prepared to take you wherever is necessary so you may study your Greek in sunshine and verdant beauty."

"Are you studying Greek?" Mrs. King asked Kate, sounding as though Kate's hobby couldn't be accurate.

The woman was friendly enough, but her presumptions about them were beginning to irritate Violet. Of course, so was the sound of the laughing children, the click-clack of footsteps, the pitter-patter of rain, and endless, debilitating chill.

Vi told herself that she was in a foul mood because she was ill and that was all there was to it, but she was afraid she was rather inclined to hate this town. The reasons why made her shift as though she had been the one to buy a house drunk, so Violet was trying to keep them to herself and find things to love.

She hated it though. She hated this house because it was too far from Jack, which would eventually make her choose between spending her time with the man she loved or the other half of herself. Each of the choices was untenable. Why! Why was her brother so stupid as to buy a house so far from Jack's historic home? His family had owned that house for generations—him buying somewhere else wasn't an option. And yet Victor—Victor who could have purchased anywhere had to buy drunk and alone when Violet wasn't able to point out the obvious result.

Kate explained that they had just returned to the country from several weeks in Cuba where Kate had become friends with a Greek fellow and his wife. She'd picked up the desire to learn the language from them. If anything, Kate's story seemed to set the local woman off even more so. She glanced them over as though they were quite foreign.

"Cuba?"

"It's lovely there," Kate said calmly.

Violet pressed a hand to her forehead and Victor noted it immediately.

"Whatever would bring you to Cuba?" Mrs. King demanded, ignoring Vi's wilt.

Victor pulled Violet to her feet and said in an aside, "A little article about rum cocktails."

Violet closed her eyes. The village had already been talking about them and the way Victor had purchased the house. They were going to get the reputation for being endlessly zozzled and frivolous.

"It *was* lovely to meet you, Mrs. King." Kate smiled graciously. "I so look forward to visiting those places you mentioned. And to hear that you have such a nice bookstore. I fear I will haunt it daily. We should get Violet to bed before she collapses. The auto is ready?"

Victor nodded and said his farewells. Violet tucked her hand through the crook of his elbow. "You're already known for being endlessly drunk."

Victor didn't seem bothered. "I did buy the house while I was in my cups. I fear it was an inevitable conclusion. Shall we see what I've done?"

THEY SAW a rolling green lawn first with a low hedge that lined the boundary. The gardener turned onto a drive and slowed. As he moved towards the house, Violet took in hedges shaped into mystical creatures. They seemed to be green honor guards to whomever might want to visit Victor's house. Violet gasped as she took in the sight of a hedge made into a bear. The next was a mermaid and then a griffin.

Violet shook her head at the perfect, sheer frivolity and turned to Victor. "How bad can the house be if this is the drive?"

He didn't seem as confident based off of the garden. Violet didn't quite realize the house had come with so much land, and she guessed that Victor hadn't known either. He looked a little wild about the eyes as the auto finally stopped.

The house was gray stone with a new red roof. It had several steps down and gargoyles on either side of the house. There were matching ones on the roof. This was no mere cottage in the country. She counted a good half dozen windows on each side of the house. This was a home you needed to actually manage.

Victor's expression was solemn as he took it in. She knew he'd prefer some little place near the sea over this thing. Was he feeling the choke of chains weighing him down? Actual responsibility? Was her future going to include taking care of this as well? Victor wasn't one whose mind wanted to linger long on linens and tree-pruning, and yet there were probably dozens of rooms inside and definitely orchards on either side of the house.

The gardener glanced back at the three of them in the car. There was a smirk about his lips, and Violet was sure he was used to the reaction his creation caused. The gardens *were* astounding. He hadn't missed Violet's gasp as she'd taken them in, and his gaze settled on her. He wasn't expecting praise. He seemed to think she didn't note his gaze, and she felt almost as if he were stripping her bare.

She met his gaze and raised a brow. With a scowl and a bit of bite in his voice he said, "There's a daily servant here to help you get started. The butler and housekeeper retired when Mrs. Higgins died. Wasn't able to find anyone else. Not really my place."

Violet rubbed her brow. "Do you know of anyone who might be interested in the position?"

The gardener shook his head again. He was so blithe in his response, Violet felt as though he'd kept a name back. She knew she was irritable, but the way he shrugged and gestured to the house didn't make her like him in the least.

Victor had opened the auto door and handed out Kate and Violet. She walked up the steps and Giles—Victor's gentlemen's gentlemen— opened the doors.

"Bless you, Giles," Violet said, sneezing again and then moaning a little. "How bad is it?"

"Not too bad, my lady," he said. "Your man of business has the place up and running. The furniture arrived. It looks fresh and new for the most part. I suspect that they had to get rid of most everything."

Violet nodded. "To be honest, I would just very much like a bed. I'll explore later. Did Beatrice find my room?"

"Indeed, my lady. Beatrice has been rushing with the daily girl to get the beds made up, fires started. The house doesn't have central heating. The gardener really should have at least lit the fires."

Violet didn't care as long as her room was ready. "Kate will take care of whatever needs to be done. I'm sorry, love."

"Go lie down," Kate ordered. "Victor and I will see to everything."

Violet walked up the steps and down the hall. There was a master bedroom, a bedroom for the lady of the house, and three more excellent bedrooms. Violet took the room that had the things she'd ordered for herself when they'd been buying furniture. She'd selected wallpaper, carpet, and furniture. It had been the first time she'd been able to decorate a bedroom for herself since having money of her own, and she'd had fun even if she had been rushed.

At that moment, however, she sent a cursory glance over the room while she dropped her wet things. Her room was grey and black with lavender accents. The bed was a black canopy with dragons carved into the head and footboard. The quilt was entirely grey with deep purple embroidery to create Chinese style dragons.

The fire was crackling merrily, and the bed had been made with the covers pulled back. Beatrice had pulled out a heavy nightgown and robe, and she popped out of the closet. "Oh, there you are, my lady. I thought you might like a bath? I have everything ready if you wish."

"Goodness yes," Violet agreed. "A bath, a nap, tea?"

"Letty is making it. She agreed to stay on while we're here."

"Bless you. Ask her about housekeepers and give the names to Victor." A wicked yawn had Violet grabbing onto the wall while her world went askew. A moment later, she tried and failed to shake off the approaching cloudiness.

The bath was an ivory clawfoot, but the faucet was a dragon. Violet grinned at it, knowing Victor had selected it for her as a

13

surprise—a fanciful faucet to match her bed frame. Beatrice had already started the water. Violet could smell mint in the salts, and with it, the pressure in her head was fading.

Violet sank gratefully into the water and whimpered when the heat settled into her. It was so hot, it almost hurt, but still felt as though it could be hotter. Beatrice nudged Violet through a full cup of tea that had been doctored with whiskey at Victor's insistence, and then Violet slipped into her bed and sleep.

She woke to someone asking, "She's sick?"

In the vaguest of ways, she recalled a discussion over her bed, a man with cold hands who looked into her eyes and touched her forehead. She sat up, pushing back her eye mask. With a gasp, she stared up at Jack, who grinned at her. She sneezed in reply, moaned, and he touched her forehead. "You've got a fever, love."

He held out two pills and another whiskey, with Victor looking on. Violet touched her nose, knowing it was red. No doubt she had bags under her eyes. She had no desire for that cup Jack was waving under her nose. "You'll need to sleep the day away, I think."

"You're here?" she asked stupidly.

"It's been days, darling," he said.

She pressed her hand to her forehead and flopped back onto her pile of pillows. Violet tried and failed at shoving the mug away. "What day is it?"

"Thursday." He grinned at her pitiful self. "How do you feel?"

"Awful."

His hand was careful on her head as he said, "You do look woeful."

"You've slept for days, you lazy thing," Denny called from the hallway. "Haven't you expired from lack of food?"

Violet curled onto her side. Why did she have such an audience when she felt so bad? She shivered and pulled the covers around her neck. "Go away, you fool, Denny. You were sick when I left London. I know you were. This is your fault."

"Only I feel like a million bucks now, luvie. Now that you're back to the land of the living, you'll get well quickly. Eat something. It'll make the headache better."

Violet cast a pleading look at Victor, who called for Beatrice and shuffled everyone else out.

"Oh, my lady."

Violet drank the mug of tea and whiskey, giving into Beatrice's militant gaze. As Violet did, Beatrice chattered about the new house-keeper who looked just like Hargreaves and the housekeeper's very proper husband. Victor had apparently called Jack and had him bring down Hargreaves's family to fill the post of butler and housekeeper.

"No one local would take the positions. Can you imagine?" Beatrice asked as she tucked a warmed brick into the end of Violet's bed and stoked up the fire. "The gardener is not well-liked, and the few who applied declined the positions when they heard that he was still working here."

Violet gasped and then her breath caught on a cough. The racking attempt to recover her breath left her curled on her side. Beatrice rubbed Violet's back until the coughing fit ended.

"…the gardens *are* lovely, though I haven't had a chance to explore them at length. They aren't even the award winners, my lady. As lovely as they are here, there are even nicer gardens in this village."

Violet focused on her breathing, and when she listened to the girl again, Vi heard, "…and then Mr. Victor rang up Mr. Jack and Mr. Hargreaves. Since Mr. Victor couldn't find anyone local…"

Violet let the flow of Beatrice's chatter flow over her and only half-listened.

"I went to the local store to get the vapor rub, my lady. Mr. Victor had Mr. Giles take me when I told him I was going. While I was there, I was fair questioned within an inch of my life. How long we were staying, how much you drink, how rich you were. It was shocking."

"You loved it." Violet laughed.

"I did," Beatrice confessed. "I told them I rarely saw you drink heavily, and they about died, thinking I was lying. Well, I never! The story of Mr. Victor buying this house while intoxicated is town legend, my lady. Nothing I could say would counteract that."

Violet laughed into her pillow. "It serves him right for being so foolish. Is it a nice village? I only have the vaguest recollection."

"I'm sure anyone would be happy to live here."

Violet fell asleep while Beatrice talked. When she woke again, she was alone. Vi slowly sat up, peeked out the window, and saw that the sun was just rising. Had she slept another day?

She sniffed and her nose wasn't clogged anymore. Violet hesitated to think she might be better, but when she crossed to her bath, her head didn't pound with each step. She scrubbed her body and realized that she was starving. She stretched out her legs, arms, and back carefully in the bath and then dressed herself. It was spring, but Violet wasn't quite ready to wear a light pink chiffon dress in fear of catching another chill. Instead, she put on a blouse, a deep green pleated skirt, and a cardigan.

The clock had struck 8:00 a.m. by the time she finished dressing. Surely someone would be up and there would be something to eat? She cleared her throat as she left her room, checking to see if it hurt, and one of the other bedroom doors opened.

Jack smiled at her. "She has risen!" He was dressed fully and looked dapper indeed with his pin-striped grey suit and shiny shoes. He took her hand, looming over her, and she was reminded once again how very large he was. Something of a mountain in human form with penetrating eyes and dark coloring.

"I feel as though I could fly," Violet confessed, leaning on his arm. She wasn't quite sure how long it had been since she had eaten, but she longed for a feast.

He laughed as he took her hand, lifting it to his lips and pressing a kiss on her knuckles. She shivered, but it had nothing to do with having a chill. "There's nothing quite like feeling better after being ill. The difference is so astounding that you just might mistake your capacity."

Violet shot him a condescending look. "Is that your way of saying I should still take a nap today?"

"It is, indeed. You might also wait a few days before you try out the bicycles your brother purchased."

Violet glanced up at him, taking in his face, and felt as though all must be right again. She was feeling better and her massive Jack had arrived. Violet had become used to having Jack around nearly all the time and discovered that was just how she preferred it.

"This is when I admit that I went straight to bed and have no idea where we might find breakfast."

Jack's shoulders shook with silent laughter, but he led the way without teasing her. She looked around the house with delight. She'd imagined quite the grimmest outcome.

Instead, the wooden floors had been freshened and shone in sunlight that came in through bright windows. The walls were freshly papered and the simple colors set off the paintings Victor had sent down to enliven the walls. To Victor's amusement, the previous owner had left the family portraits, so Vic had told the clerk to merge the two families on the walls.

"It isn't so bad," Violet breathed out, her relief readily apparent.

"I was a bit surprised at how nice it was. I wonder how much was nice to begin with and how much was the fellow you sent down here to sort it out?"

CHAPTER 3

*V*iolet yawned over her weak tea until Jack dragged her back to her room and told her to nap. Her throat was aching and her eyes were watery when she lay back down. She woke again when someone entered her bedroom.

"Hello, darling." Victor sat on the edge of her bed. She ran her fingers through her hair and rubbed her eyes. "Are you feeling quite the thing?"

"I feel like a wrung out dishrag." She twisted a kink out of her back. "I smell like a bag of peppermint candies and sweat. That *is* delightful, isn't it? Rather becoming and whatnot. But I do feel better, I suppose. Denny, damn him, was right about eating something."

Victor flicked her with a pencil and said, "I've started a sensational novel without you and realized it's always you who starts them. I never understood the first part of the book was quite so hard."

There was a little bit of a whine to Victor's voice, but Violet shrugged it off. She supposed that she was reading too much into every little thing. She was just irritable from being ill. Vi sniffed to check if her nose was still clear and just kept herself from breaking into a hallelujah chorus when she could breathe.

"Why did you have to import servants? Won't it rather dispose the locals to dislike us even more?" It was the wrong thing to say. She saw it immediately when his jaw tightened and the usual versions of him she knew—the spaniel and the lion—were displaced by the mule. She sighed and his eyes sharpened on her face.

"Are we so bothered by what a bunch of local...local...yahoos think of us?" Victor's eyes approached actually being wild. Violet wanted to growl in reply to his expression but told herself to contain herself.

"I—"

"No doubt you could have done better," he said and then sneezed. "You do everything better. Write our books, run Agatha's business, keep track of our investments."

Violet bit her lip. Irritable? Check. Sneezes? Check? Flushed cheeks? She examined him and noted the pale skin with brilliantly red cheeks. She sighed once again but tried and failed to hide her reaction. Sick Victor made rabid rodents seem pleasant.

"Victor..."

"Save it," he snapped. "If you feel up to it, your lover is here, haunting the halls, waiting for you to come down."

"Victor..."

"If you don't distract him," Victor snarled, "I'll have to commit a murder to distract him myself. Then there's Kate, who hasn't seen you since you disappeared. She has been running the house in your stead. You better hurry getting out of that bed or you'll miss her. Mrs. Lancaster is disposed to think us a pack of fools and is ready to draw her home."

Violet winced. She could only imagine how much that would upset healthy Victor, let alone childish, stubborn, sick Victor.

"Even Lila and Denny are past ready for you to appear."

Violet pressed her lips together as Victor slammed the door. She shouldn't have said what she had and she'd have apologized immediately, but instead, he'd lashed out.

"It's just because you're still getting better," she told herself as she angrily wiped a tear off of her face. "He didn't have to be quite so awful."

Violet wasn't going to go chasing after the...the...jackass! She was going to take a bath and resolve the issue of her fragrance. She hauled her body out of bed, wincing at the stiffness and added lavender bath oils to the water. She sank into the water, holding herself under until her lungs burned but her eyes had finally stopped shedding.

The dinner gong was going to ring before long, so Violet put on one of her new dresses. It was blush pink with a diamond accent under her chest. As angry as she was with her brother, she left her black pearls and selected a diamond collar and bracelets with diamond bobby pins in her hair. She hesitated before she took a silk wrap. Her dress was sleeveless but not particularly low cut in either in the front or the back. Even still, she wasn't sure how well she'd last without something to keep her warm.

Violet walked down the stairs and found that she was the first to arrive. She examined the walls, frowning at the oil painting of her and Victor. It was next to a family she'd never seen, but the painter had certainly captured the woman's sour mouth. Violet raised a silent, imaginary glass to the artist and wondered if she could get him to do one of Victor.

Maybe the painter could somehow perfectly encapsulate the stubborn, nasty version of him that Violet knew would stick around until he finally got over his illness. Speak of the devil! He walked into the room a moment later. She scowled at him, and he frowned at her. Their dogs went running through the room a moment later before Beatrice chased in after them. They both turned to her, and the twins' expressions made her pale. She grabbed each dog under their belly, curtsied, and fled without a word.

"You've upset my maid." Violet straightened the picture of the sour old woman and decided it was going home with her. She'd hang it outside of her bedroom as a warning to her brother to not bring out her inner devil.

Jack walked into the room a moment later and found the twins glaring. "Ahh..."

They turned on him and he held out his hands in surrender and sat, crossing his legs.

"I suppose you want a drink?" Victor demanded with a sneeze.

Jack glanced at Violet, who walked to the window and stared out. It was dark and there was nothing to see but the reflection of her brother pouring a gin-heavy cocktail.

"I think I'll pass," Jack said cheerily. The cheer was forced and nearly as awkward as the anger springing between the twins.

"What's this I hear about a gardener who isn't safe around Beatrice?" Violet knew she shouldn't ask the question as she formed it. This time, however, she did it deliberately.

Victor turned on Violet and she smirked back. His gaze narrowed on hers, and she sat, slowly crossing her ankles. She lifted one brow and waited. His cheeks were ruddy, and she guessed he was running a fever. He was such a child about being ill. At least Violet could be counted on to hide away until she was feeling better. Victor, on the other hand, turned into a man-monster, making everyone around him miserable.

Kate entered next and with her Lila and Denny. Kate was wearing a black beaded gown that was divine with her bright eyes and clever smile. Violet winced at her arrival. Kate was about to meet the worst version of Victor, and Violet had wound him up.

"Hullo, Kate." Because Vi was feeling her own inner-monster, she added, "I've hauled myself out of bed to take the burden of running the house off of you."

Kate grinned and then seemed to catch the feeling in the air.

"Oh, by Jove!" Denny looked at the twins and crossed to the bar. "Come, come Kate, Lila, we'll need to drink heavily if these two are sniping at each other."

"I apologize for abandoning you while I was *ill.*" Violet's emphasis simply made Victor frown harder at her. "Have you been bothered by the terrible gardener?"

Victor's glass clinked down heavily as the dinner gong rang, cutting off whatever he was about to say. Violet winked at her brother in his fury which deepened his fever-flush and reached even the tips of his ears.

Jack handed Violet to her feet, tucking her close before her brother could strangle her. "What's all this?" Jack's question was low enough that only Violet could hear.

"Victor scolded me. We're in a snit. Stand clear." Vi didn't bother to lower her voice, and Victor growled and then coughed into his handkerchief. "Also, sick Victor is a bloody bastard who lashes out. Be prepared. The man you know is gone and even the schoolroom version of him would find him churlish."

Jack seated Violet at the foot of the table and took the seat to her right. Kate sat next to Victor with Lila and Denny across from each other. Violet had never been in the dining room, but some of the table leaves had been removed, so it was easier for the twins to scowl at each other.

"I am not sick." Victor's glassy eyes met hers in a near rage, and she raised her wine glass in mockery before taking a sip.

"If he's sick..." Jack was clearly going to advise Violet to patience and understanding. That wasn't, however, how things worked when the twins fought. Violet never, ever let Victor treat her poorly, which he only ever did when he was sick.

"Then he'll learn."

"Ah." Jack coughed back a laugh.

"Drink up, my lad." Denny topped off Jack's wine glass. "You'll need it."

The shock on Kate's face was almost as surprising as Victor's blush when he noticed her reaction. He was drinking whisky, which told Violet he knew he was truly sick. They'd had the post-illness apology session enough times to be certain he also knew how he was behaving.

Their gazes met and a silent conversation darted between the two of them. Violet's expression accused him and his was the sort of guilt-filled acknowledgment that he knew he was being horrible but that nothing was going to change.

"Victor..." Kate's hiss wasn't *quite* low enough, and he turned his ferocious frown on her. He jumped a moment later, and Violet was almost positive that Denny had kicked Victor before he could ruin things between himself and Kate. He tried smiling at her but she seemed unappeased.

Jack took up the conversational gauntlet as Victor turned his scowl on Denny. Between the two friends, they kept Victor from completely throwing his life to the hounds. When dinner was finished, Kate turned on the wireless and Victor fell asleep in an armchair. Violet left them all to wander the room, trying to fight off her anger at her brother, but it wasn't working.

She glanced outside, saw figures shadowed against the lawn and wondered if the gardener was really working this late. She almost turned to ask about the man again, but the sight of her brother having succumbed to sleep and her friends whispering to each other around his fitful form kept Violet from speaking.

From what she'd seen of it, the house was nicer than she expected. The good bones that Victor had bought had taken well to the updating they'd arranged. It was a house that anyone would be proud to own, the gardens were enough to stop you in your tracks, and Violet hated it. She scowled at her reflection and hoped her feelings about the house were caused only by being ill and by Victor's behavior.

She tried to imagine the next round of holidays in this house and shuddered. It didn't matter that the furniture was new and she'd chosen much of it. It didn't matter that the floors were gorgeous or the paper had been well hung on the walls. There was just something about this house that was turning her away, and she couldn't quite pinpoint what was causing her feelings.

CHAPTER 4

The next day dawned bright and blue, and Violet rose feeling even better. Certainly the excess of sleep was contributing to her current feeling of euphoria.

The breakfast room was empty when she arrived, but she had her new journal, a new fountain pen, and some time to gather her thoughts. The sun shone through the French doors and Vi glanced outside. A quick memory of the sculpted hedges struck her.

With the sun shining and her feeling so much better, Violet felt it was time to step outside. She ended up leaving by the front door because she didn't know where the back or side doors were. The gravel of the drive had been recently raked and the flower beds and massive flower pots were abounding with early blooms. Violet leaned down to sniff one of the flowers, which didn't smell nice at all. The scent definitely didn't match the flower's looks.

The path around the house was carefully laid with grey bricks that matched the home. The birds were singing and Violet spied one that was swooping in to land for another worm. No doubt there was a nest nearby. Was it too early in the season for hatchlings? She really had no idea.

She walked towards the back garden and paused. Victor and Kate were walking there on the green. He was just lifting her hand to his mouth, and she was looking up at him through her lashes. Violet wasn't sure that there was anything that could show true love more than the way they were looking at each other, and she wasn't going to interfere. As much as the spiteful side of her demanded revenge, Violet wasn't quite that petty.

She turned and tiptoed away and could only hope that her dog, Rouge, didn't catch her scent. The dog would come belting towards Vi, barking joyously and then Victor and Kate would expect her to join them.

She was smirking as she crept away and then once she was out of sight, she took off towards the other end of the house. As she went pelting past, the front door opened and Jack stepped out. He caught her running, and she put her finger to her lips as he settled his fists on his hips.

Vi winked and then darted to the other side of the house. A second later, she heard him chasing after. Violet swung around the side of the house just before he caught her and then darted towards the small orchard. Perhaps if she could get among the trees...a moment later, she felt his arms wrap around her, and she was pulled off her feet.

Jack's mouth was pressed into her ear as he asked, "What are we escaping?"

Violet wiggled until he set her down. "Romance."

"Romance?" His gaze narrowed on hers.

"Victor's," she expanded. "Love is in the air. Sisters are unwanted. Even twin sisters. Besides he'll probably turn back into a vicious child if I'm around."

Jack's face cleared a little bit. "I'm afraid I heard him coughing this morning. Too proud to take to his bed?"

"Pride has nothing to do with it," she said. "Vic just hates being ill and is too much of a fiend to be persuaded into anything. Are we bicycling and having a picnic today?"

He felt her forehead. "We were all waiting to see if you were well enough. With Victor ill..."

25

"I think perhaps I will be well enough, but I am afraid there is no persuading Victor to sense."

"Perhaps not too far for you then," Jack said firmly.

"Are you being protective?" she teased.

"Get used to it, luv," he told her seriously and took her hand. "Did you eat?"

"I got full after a piece of toast."

"You need to eat," he told her.

Violet ignored him and reached up to run her fingers over the apple blossoms. "Have you explored the town at all?"

He shook his head. "Lila and Denny went into town and were scolded by the pastor when he caught Denny kissing Lila. They were quite out of the way, not in the middle of the road. To hear Denny tell it, they were scolded as though they'd been discovered streaking naked through the green."

"We're scandalous," Violet told him. "It's Victor's fault. We can be nothing other than drunk, rich, idiots after the way Victor purchased this place."

"Only sometimes," Jack laughed. Something caught his attention and Jack frowned. Violet turned to follow his gaze, but she couldn't quite see what he was seeing. He was unfairly taller than her, she thought.

Jack placed his hands on her waist and lifted her. The orchard ended with hedges that faded into a wood. The gardener, Philip, was leaving the wood with a woman trailing after. Her dress was askew and she was saying something to Philip that had him turning and making a sharp movement.

Violet gasped as Jack set her down and pulled her into the shadow of a tree. They pressed together out of sight as Philip went stomping past. He was a good ways down the orchard, far enough that he didn't notice his audience. The woman followed after and he turned suddenly. Violet bit her lip to keep silent when Philip took the woman's hand and yanked her to him. He pressed quite a violent kiss on her, but she didn't object. The gardener said something into her ear and then hurried out of sight.

Violet watched unashamedly as the woman straightened her dress. She smoothed back her hair. She calmly let her mussed hair down, ran her fingers through it, smoothing the locks. A quick twist of the wrist later, and it was in a precise knot at the base of her neck. A moment later, she pulled out her compact and updated her soft peach lipstick. Pasting a smooth expression on her face, she transformed herself from Aphrodite to a conservative country woman. Once she was put back together, she hurried back into the wood.

"There must be a trail back there," Jack murmured.

"There must be someplace to have an assignation back there," Violet added, shaking her head with admiration on how easily the woman had adjusted her look. Violet would never have been able to go from scandalous to respectable so easily.

Jack's voice was a little husky when he asked, "Shall we go find it?"

Vi gaped at him, and he laughed.

"You tease!" She smacked his chest. She guessed, however, if she said yes…well…no. He wouldn't take her to some just-used place in the woods. If she let him know she wasn't unwilling, how would he react? Did she want to…?

Jack watched her face and then tucked her under his arm, enjoying the shadows with her.

Violet blushed at the thought and then deliberately changed the subject. "I understand that there is a rose garden here somewhere. Something truly lovely. We met a woman at the train station who was irritated that we might not be caring for it properly."

Jack took her hand and kissed her fingertips, not seeming to mind the awkward transition from assignations to rose gardens. She looked up at him, smiling, and they rounded the home. She had this surreal moment where she realized that she and Jack had echoed the same movements of Kate and Victor not long before.

When Violet had witnessed her brother's love, she had thought they seemed to be the perfect example of love, and yet she and Jack weren't so different. The problem was that Violet was certain Victor was in love and she wasn't as certain of Jack's feelings.

It was at the back where the rose gardens rolled out. Double doors headed down from the house with a large, covered patio. A walk extended from the backdoors to the rose garden. Violet paused in sheer, shocked appreciation. The roses were *just* beginning to bloom, but even from this distance she could see that there were a number of shades. She had no doubt that some would be called fanciful things like Queen Anne's Petticoat or Polaris' Blossom.

"If you were going to name a rose something fanciful, what would you call it?"

Jack tugged one of her locks of hair lightly and countered, "What would you name it?"

"I was just thinking that Polaris' Blossom sounds fun," she said. "You?"

"Ah...Violet's..."

She smacked his arm before he could finish. "Stop it with that piffle."

Jack took her other hand, drawing her into a dance position, and waltzed her across the garden and back to the front drive. "Shall we walk?"

"You're checking how strong I am, aren't you? Before we take up the bicycles?"

He grinned at her and winked. "Perhaps."

The walk down the drive didn't push Violet too far, but she was hiding that she was a little tired. What was he looking for? That she leaned on his arm more than usual? That she turned pale?

"Perhaps." Violet tapped her lips and scrunched her nose at him. "You can't pull the wool over my eyes, my good man. I am no bunny lost in the woods, unable to find her own way."

"You spent too much time with those Americans on the ship. Speaking of piffle, the term bunny..."

Violet gasped, fluttering her fingers against her chest and batting her lashes. "What's this now? Albert and Belinda were the bee's knees. Simply tip-top!"

Jack looked up from her and tensed. Violet followed his gaze and saw the woman from the wood. She was, however, walking on the arm of another man. The lane was narrow, so Violet could see the expressions on them. The woman was carefully blank with no more expression than a china doll. The man, however, hissed into the woman's face. Violet could see her lean just slightly back, but he didn't take the hint to stop crowding the woman.

They were walking so close together as to be clearly belonging to one another...only that man was *not* Philip the gardener. Just what had Violet and Jack witnessed?

"Oh," Violet breathed. She smiled at the couple as they drew near and called, "Good morning!"

"Well now," the man said, "you must be the folks who purchased the old Higgins place. Heard all about that." The man was about forty or so and the woman on his arm had to be near Violet's age, barely in her mid-twenties.

"Her brother, Victor Carlyle, is the homeowner." Jack held out his hand. "I am Jack Wakefield. This is Lady Violet Carlyle."

The man's brows lifted and he nodded at Vi. The woman smiled prettily at both of them, and Violet breathed out in relief that they hadn't been caught at being peeping-toms. "Joseph Baker. I'm one of the local barristers. This is my wife, Melody Baker."

Violet would never cease to be amazed at her capacity for play-acting at that moment when she grinned and held out her hand. "Delighted to meet you. We were just out catching the air. I'm afraid I have been rather under the weather and missed most of our journey through the village."

"Heavy drinking will do that," Mrs. Baker said sweetly, almost righteously. "It's better to keep drinking to the minimum. I find a strict regimen of fruit, vegetables, and exercise to keep me quite healthy."

Violet blinked at the outright cattiness delivered so sweetly and so judgmentally. It wasn't *Violet* conducting affairs in the wood, nor was enjoying alcohol so very wicked. Breaking one's wedding vows, however...and with a gardener. What would the respectable Mr. Baker think of that? "Such good advice."

Jack nodded to both of them and they walked on. The moment they were out of hearing Violet muttered, "Of all the cheek."

"These people are determined to dislike you given the way the house was purchased. They'll learn and repent. Don't worry, little love."

"I am neither worried nor little. You, sirrah, are simply mountainous." Violet shook her head. "All that snideness to our faces *and* after we caught her with another man. Do you think her husband was out looking for her because he knows she strays? Or was it just unlucky happenstance that she ran into him? Maybe that's why she keeps her lipstick in her pocket. Otherwise her husband would catch her with it kissed off and know it wasn't him who did the mussing."

"She seems like a woman who is prepared for that eventuality."

Violet snorted. "You called her loose so smoothly. You deliver a wicked barb. It is too bad she didn't hear it."

"She met you on the street and called you a lush to your face. We were never destined to be friends."

They returned to the house with a little more vigor since Violet was running on irritation. It seemed to be enough energy to set aside Jack's concerns so when Victor suggested fish and chips at the pub for lunch, Jack didn't disagree.

Violet would have if she thought Victor would listen. Even Kate's hesitation wasn't enough to get her brother to turn from his idea to have lunch at the pub. Violet watched him shiver, shook her head, and knew he was determined to dig his own grave. She was rather inclined to let him and then watch him stumble in.

"Are you sure?" Kate asked carefully, her eyes wide with concern.

Victor shrugged in reply, not even seeing the concern on Kate's face. "It's not too far, and I'd love to try whatever those fizzy drinks were again. You will adore them."

Violet smiled, trying not to wince. The first thing they'd do in the town was eat lunch and hunt up the clever bartender? They were cementing their reputation, weren't they? Jack seemed to follow her thoughts even though all she said was, "Fish and chips does sound lovely. It has simply been forever since I've had some done well."

"That does sound nice," Kate agreed, though she wasn't successful at masking her concern. Victor was too blind from his illness to note it.

Lila and Denny simply glanced at each other. They were as concerned as the rest of them, but no one objected verbally. Denny only said, "I'm always good for some chips."

"Or fish," Lila said for him.

"Or a good pint in a pub," Denny added.

"Or a box of chocolates from the shops," Lila said, poking his side. He'd expanded a bit on their last vacation. The food had been abundant and amazing. So very different from what they normally enjoyed.

Violet had been grateful to have Kate along on the trip to Cuba, speaking to the chefs and learning about the recipes. If Violet was not mistaken, when Kate wasn't buying books, she'd been buying herbs and spices to attempt duplicating the food in England. The woman really needed a cook in her household to do the heavy lifting. Victor wasn't going to want to watch his wife slave over a stove. She'd just hire some brilliant chef, especially since Kate seemed to be intrigued more intellectually than by a desire to practice herself.

Perhaps, however, Violet was reading her friend's desires wrong. Or maybe, Kate would only want to learn and then move onto learning something else. Violet guessed it might be more that last version. Violet reminded herself that Victor's desires as far as Kate's hobbies were really of little weight. Violet did hope he'd make some comment eventually, just to tease him endlessly about it.

Violet was happy about the idea just long enough for her to realize that Jack's country home was in Kent and this house was quite a ways away. A sudden horror occurred to Violet as she stared at the house. It was *too* far. She didn't want to be half the country away from her twin brother. At least not for longer than a few days here and there. The idea struck her hard and furious, and she realized just why she had been despising this house.

Violet skipped up the stairs as though pursued by the thought. This house! Oh, this house! It was too far. Jack couldn't sell his family acres to be closer to Victor. Her eyes burned and the exhaustion of being ill combined with the storm of the emotions. She changed quickly, dashing away a quick tear, scolding herself the entire time, trying to find the control to mask her reaction. Jack's gaze was too penetrating and even while sick, Victor knew her too well for her to get away with being distressed. The last thing she wanted was to be cornered and fail at lying about why she was upset. What if Jack wasn't imagining them wed as she was? What if Victor wasn't bothered by the separation? Maybe that was why he'd bought so far away.

She forced herself to focus on her clothes. She gazed into the mirror and then chucked her dress onto the end of the bed. She had already learned that one must have a heavier skirt if one was to bicycle. As long as Violet wasn't racing down a hill on the bicycle, her skirt would stay reasonably in place. Even still, Violet put thick stockings on. She had a rather heavy wool skirt, a pretty sailor's blouse that tied at her neck, and then a wool coat that buttoned at her waist, accentuating her slim figure.

She stared at her face. She was tired already. Her legs hurt, and the toast had long since been insufficient. She wanted a warm bowl of soup, some ginger wine, and a fireplace alone where she could mope about the unfair truths of the map and the distance between the two houses.

Violet selected sturdy shoes but tried to perk herself up by adding gold earbobs and a couple of rings. Those would give her something to play with when the villagers took in the party of Londoners and judged them unfairly.

Violet took long enough to apply some rouge, lipstick, and kohl. She wasn't interested in pretending to be something other than what she was for the locals. So it may have been sheer spite that had her applying the kohl heavily. There would be no way her powder would last through a vigorous bicycle ride, but the rest of her makeup should stay strong. The locals were just going to have to recognize that Violet and their friends weren't going to pretend to not like cocktails and jazz because they were considered fast here. Nor was Violet going to apologize for every drink she enjoyed because one of the locals foisted his house off on a drunk Victor.

CHAPTER 5

The gardener, Philip, was trimming a unicorn hedge when they rode their bicycles down the lane. He nodded but didn't call a greeting. Yet again, Violet felt as though she'd been undressed, and Lila's frown told Violet she wasn't alone in her feelings.

The two friends glanced at each other and Violet was sure fury lit her expression. Her anger provided her with the energy to keep up with the others. Jack looked a bit like a giant riding a Lilliputian's bicycle. His knees stuck out at an awkward angle, and she was betting he would either order himself a larger bicycle or they wouldn't be able to persuade him on another ride.

Victor's face was flushed with an unearned redness. On an average day, Victor normally wouldn't have shown signs of struggle. The sweat pouring off his forehead proclaimed his fever. Kate pulled to a stop about a mile down the lane. "Give me a moment would you? I suppose there was too much lollygagging in Cuba."

She wiped her brow while Victor coughed into his sleeve. They all watched him struggle to catch his breath. Once he stopped hacking, Jack asked Kate, "Do you need a few more minutes?"

Her gaze was carefully not on Victor when she replied. "I think I'll be able to carry on."

Violet's mouth twitched, but she turned her head away so Victor couldn't see her expression. His tight eyes told her he was struggling, and because she loved him, she wanted to shake him within an inch of his life. A wicked idea struck her as she slowed her pace. A part of her wanted to stick a stick in his spokes, but she contained herself.

When they arrived at the pub, Victor was struggling again. He was pouring sweat and his drenched handkerchief seemed to be dripping. She shook her head and glanced around the town. The pub itself was fabulous. It looked as if it had been open since Victoria reigned. It was brick with stone and a roof that had probably been replaced a dozen or more times. It looked as though it needed to be replaced again. The sign creaked in the wind.

The group of friends with their bicycles got sideways looks from every single person they passed. At first Violet felt it was because Jack was rather ridiculous on that bicycle. It took her a moment to realize it was because they were new. Everyone in this town knew each other, and their heads slowly turned as the group passed.

"You look a bit like a monkey riding a tricycle, old man," Denny told Jack.

The roadway was cobblestone and the shops were carefully tended with flowers and fresh paint for the most part. As Violet took in the scene, she saw Mrs. King a few buildings down.

"I'll be a minute," she told Jack. Vi didn't bother with Victor since they were still at daggers drawn. He sneezed into his handkerchief and staggered into the pub. "Try to get him to drink something that might kill the cold before I put him out of his misery."

Jack's lips twitched and he nodded. Violet crossed to Mrs. King. "Hello again!"

Mrs. King nodded and then glanced from Violet to the pub and back again.

Violet understood the expression. "I understand that the fish and chips are quite delightful here."

Mrs. King softened just a bit. "They are. John Eppins is brilliant in the kitchen. I think about his stew every time I have a chill. I see you're feeling better. I'm happy for it."

Violet grinned winningly, but Mrs. King didn't react to the grin. "I truly am. It was touch and go there for a while. Mostly go. I slept several days straight, but now all is well. We were thinking of going for a longer ramble tomorrow. Do you have any suggestions?"

Mrs. King softened a little more with the request for assistance in such a respectable pastime. Perhaps if Violet and Kate were seen enough with books in hand or visiting widows, the locals would stop taking note of every drink they consumed.

Mrs. King described a walk to Violet that started behind the grave-yard and wandered through the countryside. It was defined enough, she said, from steady travel not to worry about getting lost in a random wood.

"I understand you brought in Londoners to be your servants."

She'd have apologized for it if they hadn't tried to find locals first. She was about finished with not being good enough for these folks.

"To be honest, I was sick while the servants were being hired, but I understand they did try to find someone here. I…well…those who were interested were—" Violet glanced around as though someone would be eavesdropping. The truth was she wasn't sure how to say that her brother selected the long-time servant with a bad reputation over another set of locals. Either way, it felt odd. "They had some objections to the existing staff."

Mrs. King nodded. She clearly knew exactly to whom Violet was referencing. They both, however, pretended otherwise.

"I had better join my friends. I don't want to keep them waiting."

"Who have you got with you?" Mrs. King ignored Violet's edging away.

"Oh, long-time friends. I think they were even more excited than Victor to see what he'd bought."

"And are your friends also the kind to make major purchases while in their cups?"

Violet winked and pretended the pointed question was humor-filled rather than judgmental. "I fear we have very responsible friends who are far more likely to research the rainfall and the train schedules before making such a purchase. Perhaps they find us adorable?" She smiled, including herself in the drunken purchase. She tried to seem cheery and was almost certain that she seemed irritated. "I must be off. Lovely seeing you again."

Violet walked away before Mrs. King could stop her. Rather than going into the pub, she found her way to the chemist shop, made a quick purchase, tucking the parcel into her handbag, and then found her friends.

They'd taken the table near the fire, and Victor had the seat that should have left him uncomfortable with heat, but he was shivering. She met Jack's gaze, who shook his head once. Lovely. Victor hadn't fallen for Jack ordering the whiskey for him. As though he could win against Violet when he was barely functioning.

Violet grinned at the lad who'd appeared to lead her to the table. She paused him, placing her hand on his arm. "Do you see that rather tall, slim, stubborn-looking man who's clearly becoming too-well acquainted with both your fireplace and possibly also that bloke, death?"

The spotty young man nodded with a wicked grin that he was trying to fight. Violet fluttered her lashes up at the kid. He blushed brilliantly at her and then stuttered even though she hadn't asked him anything yet. "Would you mind getting my brother a hot toddy? Just put it next to him. The same with his meal. No matter what else he orders, put a bowl of your famous stew next to him. But a word of warning?"

The lad blushed again in the light of her direct gaze. "Yes ma'am. Um? Yes? How...um...what?"

"Make sure his order is correct. He's in a fine, prickly form today since he's ill and clearly should be in bed."

He nodded, blushing a deep red. "Yes, ma'am."

Violet took the seat that had been left for her, and Victor scowled her way. She turned her fiercest frown on him while Kate hummed under her breath just loud enough to catch Victor's attention before he could attack.

"I must say," Kate declared, "this village is simply delightful. I'm not sure I've liked a place as quickly as this one. The church is lovely, the gardens abound, even hanging baskets along the main street? It's rather shockingly lovely every which way one turns."

"Oh, I don't know," Denny cut in, taking her same cheery tone and ignoring the scowling Victor, who had a hot toddy placed next to him with a pint of the local ale. "I say, my lad, that does look good. May I have one of those?"

Victor started to offer his drink, shooting Violet a nasty look as he did, and she called out, "How right you are, Denny! One for everyone please."

Her brother's gaze narrowed on hers, knowing all too well she was trying to get him to drink the one she'd ordered for him. Violet made an internal bet that he'd drink the hot toddy regardless. If he didn't, she just might have Jack hold Victor down while she poured it down his stubborn, vicious throat.

Without her expression betraying her, Violet told Kate, "I was just telling Mrs. King that I'd slept for days since we last saw her. Have you been able to explore the rose gardens?"

"Kate and I went to the dress shop," Lila said, ignoring Victor's harrumph. "I forgot my stockings. Can you imagine? In the spring when things are so wet. I am quite a dunce."

Victor opened his mouth to agree, but he jumped instead. Had Kate kicked him under the table? Violet bit her bottom lip to keep back her crow of delight. If Kate could even halfway rein in the Victor run-amuck, Violet would be both astounded and amazed. She would be utterly certain it was true and abiding love between the two.

"Did you finish your investigation?" Violet asked Jack. Perhaps talk of London would—

"Course he did," Victor snarled.

—so that wasn't going to work. Not London.

Violet sipped the hot toddy that had been left next to her and debated throwing it in Victor's lap. Jack placed his hand on hers. Was he reining *Vi* in? By Jove, Violet thought, Jack was doing just that. She glanced at him, and his lips twitched as he met her gaze. She scowled back at him. She didn't have the patience for nasty Victor, and Jack thinking he could somehow control things just irritated her further.

She ordered her fish and chips and stared out the window while Victor snapped at Lila, then Jack, then Denny. The only one who escaped unscathed was Kate, who seemed to be intolerably tolerant of the fiend.

While Violet stared out the window, she saw the gardener walk past. There was a woman on his arm. She was blond, young, curvy as all get out, and utterly, shockingly beautiful. She spoke up to Philip as though pleading. What in the world was happening there?

Vi was tired of this luncheon with her brother, though she had to admit that the fish and chips were crisp and perfect. The fish flaked apart in her mouth, the chips were soft in the center, crisp on the outside, and salted just enough to remind her exactly how much she loved the things.

Violet leaned forward to watch Philip shake off the lovely blonde and step into the hardware store.

"You'll catch flies with your mouth hanging open like that." Victor's cutting tone made her want to throw something. Don't do it. Don't do it. "Did I just see you watching the gardener? Careful Jack, you'll lose my flighty sister to the servants."

Violet turned slowly and her gaze met Victor's. She could see that he knew he'd gone too far. Precisely, she set her napkin down on the table, glanced among their friends, and rose.

"I wonder," she said idly, "just how abject your apologies will be when you're back to yourself. Perhaps, if you're lucky, I'll forgive you. Then again, you've already sworn time and again to stop being a child while ill and yet here we are once again."

She left the pub before someone could stop her and went down the nearest alley so that they couldn't follow. She didn't want to hear their excuses for her brother. She could make them herself. She knew he was ill. She knew he didn't mean it. She even knew her lack of patience with the childish version of her brother made things worse. She didn't need to hear it from the well-meaning.

She stepped into the first store before someone caught up with her, and found she'd discovered the bookstore. Violet wandered its aisles. An old friend in book form might be just the thing to get her through the day. Violet found a copy of *Barchester Towers* and ran her fingers over the words. This book and the sequel had once brought both Victor and Violet to tears with their laughter.

The problem was that she needed to escape her brother with an old friend and yet—any book she'd fallen in love with, she'd shared with him. Something then that only she liked. He wasn't one for the romances. Jane, Violet thought. Yes, *Jane Eyre*.

"Hello there," Violet said. "I'm looking for Jane Eyre…oh!" Her eyes widened as she caught sight of a *Varney the Vampire*. It was so bad and so great. The little man behind the counter found Violet a copy of *Jane Eyre* while she put *Varney the Vampire, Barchester Towers*, and *Doctor Thorne* on the pile.

"Did you want me to have them delivered?"

"I would like that," Violet said, nodding. "Except for dear Jane."

"Dear Jane? Hardly…" There was a bit of a challenge in the man's gaze.

Violet lifted a brow, winked, and said, "Jane's no Varney. But…'Do you think, because she is poor, obscure, plain, and little, she is soulless and heartless? You think wrong!—She has as much soul as you,—and full as much heart!'" When Violet finished the quote she added, "There are many contenders for some of the greatest works of fiction, sir, and I won't dispute with you regarding the placement of *Varney the Vampire* or my beloved *Bulldog Drummond*, but you and I shall come to blows over *Jane Eyre*."

His mouth twitched and he held out his hands placatingly. "Apologies, madam. I should have known better. I am, I fear, less entranced by mad wives locked in the attic and being lost on the moors than you young people."

Violet grinned as she saluted with her copy of *Jane Eyre* and tucked the book into her bag. "Perhaps you would enjoy her more if you recognized that little and plain though she might be, Jane Eyre is a heroine to give one pause and perspective."

"I concede, alas, I concede. I suppose I prefer my heroes to be men of honor. You may enjoy your funny little romance without a fight."

"That, my friend, is where you are wrong. Very little is without a fight for a woman in these modern times. You are a man among men for delivering my goods even with your poor taste in protagonists. Thank you!"

Violet stepped away from the shop before she lost her temper, glancing about to ensure that no one was looking for her before she continued her solo exploration of the village.

CHAPTER 6

*V*iolet adjusted her bag across her body as she glanced down the street. It was a leather satchel designed for men, but Violet appreciated being able to carry more than a compact and lipstick. She sighed, thinking of her friends and then hoped that Kate was scolding Victor and nudging him through his hot toddy and stew.

Violet spied the church, beyond which was the graveyard bordered by a wrought iron fence. She made her way towards the graveyard at a smart clip. She approached with half-glances over her shoulder, knowing she should go back and also knowing she wasn't going to return to accept Victor's bad behavior any time soon. She knew that sooner or later her friends would come after her. They were probably letting her cool down before they tried to talk sense into her.

The church held center court in the village with the bell tower shadowing the graveyard and the cobblestone street. The tips of the wrought-iron fence around the graveyard didn't end in the typical spade or arrow. Instead, they had been formed into lilies. Violet ran her fingers over them and made her way through the gate. There was something so peaceful about graveyards, a sense of stillness that filled the air where even nature herself seemed to stand respectful.

Many of the graves had tall crosses, but a few were looked over by stone angels. She paused under a particularly shocking angel. The angel's hard gaze was narrowed down on a string of graves with more of an avenging pose than a welcoming one.

Violet's brows lifted as she took in the attacking stance and then read the names of the graves guarded by the stone protector. Annabelle Jones, 17 March 1917 - 29 March 1920. Violet flinched for the parents. Then she gasped as she read Ethan Jones, 2 April 1916 - 29 March 1920. The same year! Down the row, she read the names and dates on four graves. Somewhere in this village, there were parents who had lost *four* children on the same day.

"A terrible tragedy," a voice said from behind her.

Violet gasped and whirled, holding a hand to her chest. "Oh!"

"Oh, I am sorry my dear. They're my nephews and niece. Little angels, they were. We suffer still for them these years later."

"I'm so sorry for your loss." Violet looked down on the fresh flowers and then up at the man. He wasn't so old. Perhaps in his mid-30s with hair just starting to thin, a powerful build, and soft blue eyes. She smiled at him, and he smiled back at her.

"My sister's children, but they felt as though they could have been mine. Annie could already sing like an angel at three years old. She'd just turned three as you see."

"I..." Violet played with her ring, helpless to know what to say.

"It's all right." The man leaned down to put flowers on the last grave. "You don't have to try to comfort me or provide perspective. I know it's a tragedy. I know our loss was steep. I know they are with God. Your expression...that's all that I need."

Violet nodded helplessly and then held out her hand. "Violet Carlyle."

"Joseph Freckleton."

"Lovely to meet you. My brother just bought the old Higgins place, so we've just come to visit."

"Ah." His lips curled in, and Violet was sure Mr. Freckleton was hiding a wide grin.

"Yes, that one. He bought the place, sight unseen, while zozzled. It seems he didn't do so badly. What a lovely place this village is and what an amazing garden. I understand that there are even more lovely gardens here."

"There are indeed. It is my sister's husband who works for your brother. She married quite...low. Philip Jones. He's the gardener."

Violet's gaze widened. Imagining the man who'd made her uncomfortable as a father. These were the graves of *his* children. "He's quite talented." She wasn't quite able to hide her reaction to the comment.

"That he is," Mr. Freckleton agreed with a smooth face. This was an educated man in front of Vi. He might be in a different class from herself, but she imagined there had been quite the row when his sister determined to marry a gardener. Violet could almost see it. Not for herself, but she could tell by the way that others reacted to Philip that he was a man many women found attractive. Attractive enough to dive through the classes?

Was she being terribly snobbish? Wasn't the reason women had fought so hard was to be able to pursue their lives as they wanted? If Mr. Freckleton's sister had wanted to marry someone that her family hadn't approved of, wasn't that her choice? Violet told herself it was and pasted a smile on her face. She hoped that her internal reflection hadn't translated to her expression.

"It was lovely to meet you, Mr. Freckleton," Violet said. "I hope that you have a delightful day. I wonder if you might show me the way to the rambling walk on the other side of this graveyard."

Mr. Freckleton nodded and showed Violet the way to the walk.

She should, she thought, go back to her friends, but she still was unable to persuade herself to do so. She was tired of facing her brother's venom and knew that if she went back, he'd lash out at her. She was going to wander through the wood, find her way to the little lake, make some terrible sketches, and visit with Jane Eyre.

The path rolled out almost eerily. Clouds had crossed over the sun, and the already cool day had turned a little chilly. Violet tucked her coat tighter about her neck and huddled into herself as the wind picked up. The path was hard-packed dirt, and even with the recent wetness was still firm. The way had been cleared so well that there weren't things growing across the path or obscuring which way to go.

It seemed to parallel the street in the village and ran up behind houses and gardens a hundred meters in.

Violet made her way down the path. The trees were just starting to blossom, and the pink buds overhead made it seem as though she'd entered a fairyland even with the deep shadows between the trees. Maybe because of them, the magic seemed to thicken. Fairyland was rather a mysterious place, wasn't it, with hollows that just might lead one to their doom or little nooks where fantastical creatures might live.

Violet reached up to grab one of the blooms and tucked the stem into the bobby pin she used to hold her hair out of her face. Normally she held her hair back with a headband or hair piece, but she'd tucked back the loose locks with bobby pins to keep it out of her face while she rode the bicycle.

She felt a flash of regret for leaving her bicycle for the others to deal with, but Violet was sure that they could pay some local lad to ride it back to the Higgins house, and she felt as though Victor deserved the headache. Though, now that she thought of it, he probably had quite a terrible one.

She made her way between a series of bushes to say hello to some horses that were in a field nearby. A dappled grey walked over and nickered at Violet, who clucked back. The horse thrust its head over the gate, and Violet scratched the fellow just below his ear.

What a lovely beast. She glanced down, noted the sex, and said, "Aren't you the prettiest man?" She hadn't had a horse of her own since she was a girl, and she suddenly missed one terribly. Dogs were lovely creatures and she hadn't realized she'd love Rouge quite as much as she did, however, horses were just so...brilliant.

Violet scratched him well and placed a kiss on his nose. He neighed at her and she laughed into his gaze.

There was a sound in the distance and both she and the horse started. Violet listened carefully. Was someone else on the path? Perhaps this fine boy's owner coming home the back way?

Her heart began to inexplicably race and the horse snuffled, eyes rolling. Violet hoped it was her fear setting off the horse and not something that he sensed that she couldn't. This is a safe little town, she told herself, stepping back onto the path after patting the horse again. He neighed at her again, but it sounded a little different.

The change scared her, making her heart speed even faster. She hurried down the path. Mrs. King had said that it came out a mere half-mile from Victor's house. Vi could hurry back home, beating her friends possibly. Maybe she'd send Beatrice down to the village to let them know Vi had returned to the house.

Violet forced her mind to focus on anything but her fear. Only… there was something on the path. Something terrible. Something shaped like a body. Her eyes widened and she turned and spun, racing away from what she'd seen. She didn't want a better look. She didn't want to face it. She didn't want a more detailed image in her mind, to haunt her later, in the nighttime.

Only…Violet stopped. She bit her lip and had to make fists before she could force herself back down the path. She had to check. To be sure.

She glanced around, taking in the scene. This portion of the trail was near the back of another house, one with roses just starting to bloom and windows that faced the trail. Any hope of putting this burden on someone else died when she saw the garden was empty.

She reached out and with shaking hands and turned the body onto his back. She noted the blood pool under his form, darkening the path. That much blood. That was no accident. It was a little harder than she realized, rolling the dead weight. Her gasp was the only sound. Staring, glassy eyes told her all she needed to know. The form truly was dead and nothing else was to be done.

The fact that she was staring at the body of Victor's gardener was even more horrifying. She'd seen him kissing a woman, she'd seen him smirking at her—snide and too knowing. She'd seen his art in the gardens. She'd seen a woman throwing herself at him. She'd even seen the graves of his children. She'd never imagined seeing him like this.

CHAPTER 7

*V*iolet ran as fast as she could go. She knew she shouldn't have left her family. She had been childish, but she'd done it and now this is where she was. She was racing through the wood by herself, trying to reach Jack before he disappeared. She gasped as she ran, hoping that her conversation with Mr. Freckleton hadn't wasted too much time. If Jack was gone, who would she turn to? The local police just felt wrong when she knew that a brilliant Scotland Yard man was around, one who knew her and cared for her.

She wanted nothing more than to throw herself into Jack's arms and shove this problem on him. She ran past Freckleton, who shouted her name when he saw her come pelting out of the wood. She passed several locals, including the Mr. Baker and Agnes King.

Violet was holding her side at that point, and her weakened lungs from her illness were struggling to let her continue. She almost collapsed in relief as she hurried up the street towards the pub, where she could still see their bicycles outside.

She pushed through the door, moving past the spotty lad who blushed at her appearance. She tried to call Jack's name, but she couldn't get words out. She heaved, her hands on her knees as Victor said something no doubt biting. Violet gasped, barely hearing her friends as she tried to speak. "Ja...Jac..."

Trying to get a word out was the wrong choice, and she broke into a racking cough that had her moaning when she finished. She took a slow breath in, realizing that Kate was slowly rubbing her back.

"Jack..." Violet huffed. "Jack..."

"I'm right here." He was a mere step away, watching Kate's movements carefully.

"Body," she coughed, wiping away the tears that had started streaming somewhere in her journey.

"Did you say body?" he demanded, voice sharp.

She nodded frantically as she coughed into a handkerchief.

"Are you sure?"

She nodded, grabbing the lapels of his jacket. "On the path....behind the graveyard." She pressed a hand against her chest where her lungs were burning and watched him jump into motion. He didn't need anything more from her than her statement. She couldn't help but consider the bookseller who'd mocked her choices in fiction. Any other man who knew her less well would have cross-examined her when they wouldn't have questioned a man further.

The boy who'd helped Violet earlier was sent for the local bobbies while Victor cursed their poor luck. Jack, on the other hand, called for a notebook from the waiter and prepared to step into his professional role.

"Stop being such a beast," Jack told Victor, "and take care of your sister."

Victor nodded, coughing into his own handkerchief while Kate wrapped Violet up in a hug, rubbing her back.

"Denny, with me. Bloody hell, Victor, get the ladies home and go to bed before one of us is forced to make you the next victim."

Victor choked on a laugh and blushed, nodding. "Vi..."

She looked up at him, her eyes welling with tears and then threw herself into his arms. She shuddered as he held her close. In his chest, she could hear him wheeze and knew she was doing the same. He said something over the top of her head, and a few minutes later, she had a drink pressed into her hand, and she was prompted to drink it while Victor ordered a car and arranged for the bicycles to be delivered.

When they reached the house, Mrs. Morganson—Hargreaves's cousin—took one look at the twins and said, "To bed with both of you. For the love of goodness, are you children?"

Violet's eyes welled with tears as she made her way up the steps. She'd added the image of a dead Philip Jones to her mind. It was seared there with the image of the four graves of his children. Of the bodies she'd seen before. Mr. Danvers dead in the library and Aunt Agatha in her coffin—it was more than she could handle.

"Violet, darling?" Lila asked. Violet jumped and turned, only realizing then that her dearest friend had followed her up the stairs. "Are you all right?"

She shook her head frantically. Lila's lovely gaze was understanding. "What do you need?"

Violet sniffed, pressing a hand to her mouth, trying desperately to hold back the flood of tears that wanted to escape. "I…"

"Tea?"

Vi shook her head.

"Coffee? I can make Turkish coffee for you?"

Violet shook her head, biting her bottom lip hard enough to feel the burn through her lip.

"Chocolates? I can raid Denny's stash for you?"

A tear slipped down Violet's cheek.

"What if I were to follow you up to your room, get you into your kimono, and read you to sleep? Something frivolous and terrible."

Violet paused and then nodded. Lila hooked her arm through Vi's. "We have the worst luck, do we not?"

Violet didn't really listen to what her friend was saying as they made their way to her room. Lila pulled back the covers on the bed while Violet changed. She didn't want to pretend to be all right, so she let Lila put her to bed instead.

Violet didn't listen to the story so much as the tenor of Lila's familiar voice. The body had been lying there in the path. Just randomly placed? How had he died? Why had he died? Violet was already filling in possible answers. Perhaps it had been how she'd seen him with two women, both of whom were familiar in how they touched him.

She recalled that the servants who'd applied to Victor's house hadn't wanted to work with Philip. Why? What was it about him that made him so objectionable? Why had Beatrice been warned to be careful? Was he the type of man who forced a girl? Or perhaps he was the type of man who made you believe he cared when he really just wanted under a girl's skirts?

Violet hadn't realized that Lila had picked up the copy of *Jane Eyre* and found the place where Vi had placed a scrap of paper. It was that same place where Jane told Mr. Rochester that she was as worthy of love and respect as he was.

What was Mrs. Jones thinking on learning that her husband had died? Was she expecting more pain after losing her children? Were there more children? Orphans now? Did Mrs. Jones know her husband was a philanderer?

"Would you murder Denny if you found out he had a lover?" Violet asked Lila, cutting into a particularly emotionally wrought scene in the book.

"Ah," Lila said, blinking rapidly. She examined Violet's face. "Would you kill Jack?"

"We aren't married," Violet said, carefully. The sheer idea that he would eventually ask her to marry him—it made her heart skip a beat. Violet sniffed and looked up as Beatrice brought a tea tray in. She left the tray and let Rouge stay in the room.

The dog leapt onto the bed and stared at Violet with soulful eyes. She wasn't sure anyone could love as purely and completely as a dog. Violet scratched Rouge's little red head and glanced up at Lila, who wasn't letting the question fade despite the interruption.

Lila stood and poured them both a cup of tea. She already knew how Violet wanted hers. A moment later, Lila returned to the bed and handed Violet her cup of tea.

"No, I wouldn't kill Jack. But I might wish I had it in me. I can't imagine how difficult it must be to keep living with someone who had betrayed you that way."

"Our mothers, aunts, and grandmothers have for centuries," Lila reminded Violet.

Vi bit her lip. "It's for reasons like that I am grateful things are changing. Think of the freedoms we have that they didn't."

"Hmmm." Lila sipped her tea before her head tilted. "Denny would never cheat on me. It's hateful of me to say that perhaps they should have chosen better."

"Especially since you know that previous generations didn't have as much freedom to choose as we have."

Violet scratched Rouge's belly as she thought over why she'd been asking the question. Lila rose and took a piece of typing paper from Violet's stack, as well as a book and a pen.

"I know you're thinking about the murder. What are you thinking? Was the gardener married? Is that why you asked about Denny stepping out on me? Or were you worried about Jack? Did he do something? What did he do? By Jove, Vi…you haven't been in bed because of something that happened, have you?"

Violet laughed at the barrage of questions and shook her head. "No, Jack didn't do anything to make me worry. He's…"

Lila smiled softly as Violet trailed off. "Very different from Denny. Perfect for you. He won't be unfaithful, I don't think. He's in love with you, but he's also honorable. You don't need to worry, Vi."

Violet squeezed Lila's hand. "You don't worry, I suspect."

Lila's brows lifted and her smirk said she knew she was adored. "But the gardener's wife? She wasn't so lucky?"

Violet shook her head and described the women she'd seen with Philip Jones, one in the orchards here and one in the village. She went onto describe seeing the graves of the children.

Lila was nibbling her lip by the time Violet finished. "He was an impetuous one with the way he eyed us. Even Denny noticed, and my lad tends to be oblivious."

Vi sneezed and held up her hand to examine herself. Had she overdone it and sent herself back to the sick bed?

"All right?" Lila asked.

Violet nodded.

With a sigh, Lila said, "I don't think we can handle you and Victor being down and out at the same time. If he doesn't have you to be a spoiled brat for, who will he strike out at next? Kate?"

Violet's expression was unimpressed. "Eventually, he'll have to shift his primary love from me to her. Then she'll get the worst of him, yes?" Violet glanced to the side, looking at her bedroom in this house. Would they eventually kick her out of it? Replace her with a child? Would she mind? Oh, she was glum, coming off of an illness. Violet needed someone to smack her out of the doldrums.

"You're acting off, Vi. Not just because of your illness, I think. Or the body. Whatever is the matter with you?"

Violet shook her head. She wasn't ready to put words to the feelings that were carousing through her. Instead, she asked Lila, "What have you written down then?"

"Wife," Lila admitted and then handed Violet the paper and pen.

Sketching out murder suspects on a piece of typing paper felt wrong, so Violet stood to get her journal instead when Denny knocked on the door.

"Vi, darling," he said. "I wonder if you might want to take Victor off of my hands. Even Kate has pled a headache."

CHAPTER 8

"*I* think this is where I apologize profusely." Victor was leaning back in his chair. His face was white while his cheeks were brilliantly red, proclaiming a fever. Violet leaned against his bedroom door, waiting for the tea tray she'd ordered to his room. She lifted her brows, silently.

"You're going to make me say it, aren't you?"

She stared blank-faced at him.

Victor flushed. He sniffed once. "I'm an insufferable ass."

Violet crossed her fingers over her stomach and waited, her heel bouncing against the hallway floor.

"I abuse you when I'm sick every time, and every time afterwards I tell you I'll be better, but I never am." He crossed to her, taking her hand and pulling her to one of the chairs near his fireplace. "I don't mean any of the nasty things I say. My head pounds, my stomach roils, I feel like I should be able to just push through, and I don't know— everything bothers me."

She cocked her head and lifted a brow as he finished his statement with a racking cough. She wasn't going to just blithely accept his apology. She just wasn't. She was well and truly tired of him acting the way he did when he was ill. The way he'd turned not just on her, but with snide comments about Jack, well...Violet didn't like that at all.

"Your cough wasn't this bad."

She uncrossed her ankles and then recrossed them the opposite way.

"It's because I didn't go to sleep immediately. I know it. Jack told me I was sick and to go to bed. Denny told me I'd owe you jewelry with the way I was behaving. I wonder if a matching black pearl bracelet would be enough."

"I can buy my own jewelry. You know what I want."

"I can't go to bed while Jack is a hunting a murderer—by Jove! Violet, this fellow killed our gardener. What if they're around here? You're here...Kate..." He stood to pace, a hand pressed against lungs she knew were burning with the effort. "You found him. What if the killer was nearby? We don't even know—"

"We don't even know if it *is* murder yet. It could be anything. Maybe it was an accident. Maybe he was ill."

"He was a strong man. I'd just seen him this morning. He caught me when I..."

Violet waited for the end of his confession, but Victor didn't finish it. No doubt, Victor had nearly passed out trying to do something he shouldn't have while ill. She was unamused, and despite his apology, she was unappeased.

Victor took the seat next to her and reached out, taking Violet's hand. "I won't lose you, Violet. You aren't allowed to be hurt or in danger when I'm around."

She laughed. She'd been in danger more than once when he'd been around.

"Don't say it! I know I can't be there every second. We should leave. We should leave like Agatha should have left when there was a killer in her home. Damn it. Damn it, Vi."

Violet winced at Aunt Agatha's name. She glanced around his bedroom, seeing it for the first time. It was blue and gold art deco with a massive black bed that she knew was brand new. He had two windows that were directed towards the gardens. Despite having an office in the house, she noticed his typewriter on a small table near his bed.

"We can't leave," she told him gently. "Jack will get called in to help. What local police force would turn down the help of an excellent Scotland Yard detective right here?"

"They might," Victor said, but he didn't sound convinced and Violet certainly wasn't convinced either.

She squeezed his hand. "There isn't any reason to believe that—if Philip was murdered—that it has anything to do with us."

Victor went back to pacing even though his lungs were rattling as he did. "The issue remains that we're here. In this house, where he spent the vast majority of his time. His murder probably has something to do with the house."

Violet shook her head. "Jack and I saw him with a married woman. It was evident, from what we saw, that they'd just been intimate. This afternoon when you—"

Victor winced. "I shouldn't have said what I did about..."

She wasn't going to excuse him. He *should not* have said what he did about Violet and the gardener. As though Violet would somehow be attracted to a man who wasn't half the creature that Jack was. Philip had made...her head tilted. He had made her feel uncomfortable from the moment she'd met him, *and* she'd been ill at that point. What if she wasn't the only one who'd been so bothered by him? What if he'd pushed someone else beyond their limits?

"I don't want Kate here around this. I should send her home."

Violet laughed at him, shaking her head.

"You don't think I should send her home?"

She rolled her eyes at him. She wasn't gentle or easy when she replied, "Has Kate suddenly become incapable of thinking for herself?"

He flushed, though it was hard to tell given the brightness of his feverish cheeks. "I..."

"You love her." Violet's tone and expression didn't give him room to hedge, but he opened his mouth to protest all the same. Violet held up a hand. She hadn't fully forgiven him, so she was snappish when she repeated, "You love her."

"I *love* you." He folded his arms over his chest, and Violet lifted a brow. He was on the edge of snapping again, and she waited to see if he'd give into it. She could see the wildness in his eyes, the frustration in his expression, the need to lash out. He coughed into his handkerchief before he said, "I'm just saying that I love you. It's not like I could possibly…be…damn it!"

Violet pressed her fingers into her forehead. He was bringing back her headache. Or perhaps it was simply the pressure of a dead body on her recovering one. "You love Kate. You want to keep her safe. With Kate, you might be able to order her home. The question is whether you'd be able to entice her out again."

Victor seemed at a loss.

"Kate is a full-grown woman who is smarter and more capable than us both."

"Me anyway," Victor said petulantly. "Why does she even put up with me?"

"You're kind and charming."

Victor grunted, and Violet rolled her eyes. As she did, Beatrice tapped on the door and stepped in with a tea tray. Her gaze met Vi's. Beatrice took in the irritated Victor and went about setting up the tray without a word.

"I don't want tea."

"You're drinking it anyway," Violet told him. She crossed to the table, turning her body to block his view, and sent Beatrice out. It was chamomile and mint tea. Violet poured something from the vial in her pocket into the teacup, added some whiskey, and then the tea with an excess of sugar. She'd have tested it to make sure her concoction wasn't too sweet, but she had no intention of sleeping the day away.

She had no patience for this nonsense on the best of days, adding in a murder to Victor's poor behavior, and Violet had reached her limits. "Victor, I am not going to listen to you whine. If that's what you want to do, by all means, try to see if Kate will indulge you. She's got stars in her eyes where you're concerned, so perhaps she won't mind."

"You're an awful fishwife. Is Jack aware you're like this?"

"Perhaps," Violet snapped, "but you can be assured that Kate has noticed your churlishness."

"You could be kinder. I was nice to you when you were sick."

"And I slept until I was well, didn't I? The worst that you can lay at my feet while ill, brother, is that our guests were neglected by me."

Victor scowled at the tea and Violet picked it up from the table where he'd set it down and placed it back into his hands.

"It doesn't taste right," he harrumphed.

"That is unfortunate. Drink it."

"I want a new cup."

"I will not make my maid who has been waiting on me hand and foot get you a new cup of tea simply because you're being a child. Drink it."

"I don't like it."

"Victor Lawrence Carlyle. Drink it or I will think of the worst stories I know of you and tell them all to Kate in a massive outpouring. She'll flee, whimpering and crying for her mother."

Victor drained the teacup in several large swallows and slapped it down on the table next to him. "Are you satisfied?"

Violet smirked at him and nodded. His gaze widened when he saw her expression. "What did you do?"

"Me?" Violet asked innocently and his entire body shuddered into a massive yawn. Violet rose and crossed to the bell pull, summoning his servant.

"When I was sick, I went to bed and you had to step in here and there. Call a doctor perhaps? Interview your own servants. For the most part, you probably played with your cocktail concoctions and smoked too much."

"Soooo..." He trailed off into another massive yawn, and his eyes were drooping. "What did you do to me, Vi?"

"Go rub your chest down with vapor rub and sleep off your doldrums before I am forced to save us all by murdering you."

"I am not a child." His eyes were watering with his exhaustion and his fight against returning to bed.

"You could have fooled me." She picked up his teacup and returned it to the tea tray, finishing the last of the tumbler of whiskey.

He stared her way and she slowly lifted her brow.

"I…"

"If you want me to forgive you, go to bed."

He yawned again and slowly stood. "I…you…"

"It's simple mathematics, Victor. I don't like you like this and no one loves you more than I do. Do you want to drive Kate away while you bound around the house making everyone miserable?"

Violet pulled back the covers on his bed and fluffed his pillows as he shuffled towards it. Giles, Victor's man, opened the bedroom door just then and Violet said, "Dear Giles, would you be a dear and steady Victor's arm? I fear he's rather overdone."

"What did you do, Vi?" Victor asked as Giles took his arm and led him to the bed.

"Take off his tie and shoes, dear Giles. Get him into pajamas if you can. I fear the laudanum is working rather more quickly than I expected."

Giles' gaze widened and he turned to stare at Victor, who was yawning around a horrified expression.

"You're welcome, brother dear. Don't come out of this room until food sounds good to you or I fear I shall be rather more direct next time."

Victor took off his suit coat as Violet crossed to leave the room. "More direct than drugging me?"

"Perhaps next time, I'll just use a blunt instrument and put you down for the count. You are welcome, brother dear. But mostly Kate is welcome. You may thank me more effusively later."

CHAPTER 9

*V*iolet left his room, laughing to herself. She should have done something like this far sooner. She hoped that finally snapping and taking matters into her own hands would teach Victor to control himself while ill. Otherwise, she really might have to find a large cage and lock him inside with broth and vapor rub.

Violet walked down the stairs and into the kitchens. Cook was working on a chicken noodle soup and some fresh bread. Violet begged a cup of tea and went into the gardens. She hadn't truly explored them and when she worked her way down the path, she paused in sheer shock. The rose bushes had been planted in a petal pattern with paths that formed the framework of each petal.

Vi hadn't bothered to look out Victor's windows but as she glanced up at the house, she was betting they looked down on this scene, allowing him to truly appreciate the splendor of the layout. There should, however, be more than one room to overlook these gardens. A wind whipped up around Violet, causing her skirt to snap against her knees, and she decided to view the garden from above until she'd grabbed her coat.

Violet wandered quite happily through the house, forcing her mind to bend towards what she was seeing rather than what she had seen. She had no desire to have her mind linger over the death of the gardener.

There was a portrait gallery that overlooked the back garden with a long balcony running along the length of the house. Violet stepped out on it and paused to take in the beauty.

As she'd imagined, the garden paths formed the lines of a rose that worked together to make a circle of petals. At the center of the circle, there was a fountain.

Beyond the rose garden was a hedge maze. To the right and left and very back of the gardens were orchards laid out in straight lines. The orchards formed a block around the garden. Because they were blooming, it was as though the garden was lined with pink and white blossoms.

She imagined the front of the house with the long drive that was guarded by fanciful hedge beasts. Philip Jones might have been a lot of things, but if there was one thing he surely was—it was an out and out genius with gardens. Had he designed this himself? Or had he executed someone else's vision? Violet very much wanted to know. She wasn't sure any garden could be lovelier than the one laid out before her, despite the tales of even finer gardens in the area.

Violet stared in awe and then turned to go back inside. Kate was waiting in the doorway, so Violet smiled a greeting.

"I wasn't sure—" Kate began.

"That you'd be welcome after my day? It was rather awful, wasn't it? Perhaps I should throw myself on your bosom and beg you to comfort me."

"Is there anything more comforting than Lila, novels, and stolen chocolates?"

"They do taste better." Violet examined Kate's face. The woman was a little pale. Her delightful freckles stood out against her face. "Are you getting ill? Or perhaps we've just made you sick with our behavior?"

Kate bit her lip. "I was afraid I couldn't be human with the way you two are so loving. You understand each other with a glance. Seeing you...ah..."

"Jabbing at each other?"

Kate pressed her lips together, but the grin still escaped. "It was rather refreshing. It feels a little as though nothing could measure up to what you two have."

Violet didn't laugh. She knew people tended to be intimidated by the twins' closeness. Especially if hopes were being laid on either twin. Women especially. Men seemed to think that Violet was both theirs for the taking and she would instantly turn all of her love and affection at whoever deigned to want her.

"Is he always so awful while ill?" Kate's voice was soft, but Violet's mostly unamused laugh was not.

"I should lie, so you'll still love him, but I'm afraid so. If you want to know what Victor was like when we were four years old and told he could not have a jam tart, well…you've just learned."

Kate laughed. "It's almost—but not quite—nice to see a little humanity from him. He's been…"

"He loves you." Violet probably shouldn't queer her brother's pitch, but sometimes a woman just needed to know she was wanted. Violet wasn't sure if Jack loved her. The more that time passed between the two of them, the more than she *needed* those words.

"Want to explore the gardens with me?"

"It feels a little…"

"Haunting? Like you're invading the land of the dead?"

Kate nodded, but they went out to the gardens anyway, staying until it was past time to come inside. They had a late tea with cucumber sandwiches, and rather than telling Kate terrible stories about Victor, Violet told Kate the best stories of him.

JACK CAME IN WITH A STORM. The skies darkened with clouds before the sunset, so it seemed as though the sun had gone down early. Violet had been reading Victor's manuscript while she waited. It was nearly time to dress for dinner when an auto stopped outside and Jack exited. He seemed to unfold and stand against the storm as some sort of otherworldly warrior. His broad shoulders didn't bow to the storm. His hair moved with the wind, but that seemed to be the only part of him that gave in to the power of it.

She heard the door open below and considered going down to him. He probably wanted to wash up and change. She didn't want to press in on his time. She tried to focus on the pages before her. She'd been trying for some time, but all she could do when she started to read was see the body of Philip Jones there on the path in front of her.

Those glassy eyes staring at the boughs overhead but not seeing. She thought about the way he hadn't been cold. She hadn't noticed it at the time, but now, she was sure he'd been warm to the touch. How long did it take a body to cool? Had she *just* missed the killer? Had the killer seen Violet discover Mr. Jones? Had the killer seen the shock and horror on her face? The fear? The way she'd run for her life as though they might strike against her as well?

Violet shuddered, feeling as though they could be watching her at the moment, even though she could be nothing more than a shadow against the glass. There would be no reason for anyone to look up at the old Higgins house, see a body in the glass, and know that it was Violet instead of any of the others. Even Victor, at a distance, might be mistaken for Violet, as slim as they both were.

"Are you all right?"

Violet turned to see Jack standing there in the hall. A moment later lightning cracked, and the electricity went out.

"Vi?"

She crossed to him, following the sound of his voice while she heard others cursing in the distance.

"Should we find candles? Or just wait until the servants find us?

Jack took her hand. He chuckled and then she felt his fingers trace up her arm, until he found her shoulder. His hand moved from her shoulder to her chin. In the darkness, his fingers traced her lips. She felt his breath against her skin before she felt his lips. They settled on hers. A moment later, she opened her mouth to him. A moment after that, he pulled back, laying a gentle kiss on her cheek, her temple, her forehead before returning to her lips. She could feel his fingers dig into her back for a moment and then heard, "My lady?"

Violet stepped back, chest heaving as Beatrice called again, "Lady Violet? Are you here, Lady Violet?"

"Here I am," Violet answered and Jack's hand fell from her back.

A moment later, Beatrice turned into the room where Violet had been sitting. She held a candle aloft as she said, "Mr. Morganson is looking into what happened with the lights, but he fears we'll be without them until the storm has passed."

"I'm sure we will," Jack said, and Beatrice gasped.

"Oh, Mr. Wakefield. I hadn't realized you returned."

"Only just," Jack told the maid. Together, the three stepped into the hall together, and the maid led the way to his room, leaving him where his man had already brought candles. "We should see about finding some lanterns."

"I'll see to it," his man said.

Violet glanced back and found Jack's gaze on her. She wasn't sure what he saw, but the weight of his gaze made her shiver. She wanted to ask him about the case. To find out if Jones had really been murdered. To throw herself back into his arms and let the strength of him make her feel safe. A feeling she didn't have any longer despite being in the house with their friends.

Instead she said, "I'll see you at dinner."

Candles always added more light than Violet expected. Her room was well-lit within moments and she applied her makeup quickly. With the flickering light, she couldn't really tell if she used too heavy of a hand with her kohl, but she doubted anyone else would be able to tell either. She didn't bother with the powder, but added a pretty red lipstick she'd picked up in Cuba.

Her dress was a sleeveless pale blue with fringe that started mid-thigh and ended above her knees. The fabric was shimmery and caught the reflection of the candlelight, making her seem as though she could have stepped out of faerie.

Violet wrapped her long strand of white pearls around her neck and considered whether it was excessive to see if she could find someone to make her a strand of pink ones. Perhaps something she should consider when Victor started talking about buying her apology jewels.

She smirked into the mirror wickedly and added some gold and diamond bangles to her wrists and some earbobs. She stood and spun in front of the mirror, watching the fringe flare and hoping that the look kept her at the front of Jack's mind.

She winked at herself, blackened her lashes, and then left her bedroom just as the supper gong rang.

"Wherever is Victor?" Kate asked when everyone else had gathered.

"I drugged him," Violet said casually. "The laudanum should keep him sleeping through the night. The rest of us should pray he wakes improved, as I'm not sure he'll be accepting tea from me again."

Denny immediately choked on a laugh, drowning out Kate's gasp. Jack's gaze fixed on Violet as she shrugged away their reactions. He didn't react at all, and for a moment she was concerned that he felt she overstepped.

"I'm surprised you didn't do it before," he said, relieving her fears.

"I fear you have to be rather unexpected with things like that."

CHAPTER 10

"*A*re you well?" Jack glanced Violet over and then answered for her, "Of course you aren't."

Her lips trembled a little. She'd tried to eat dinner, but it had all tasted like ashes. The sight of Philip's body was assaulting her mind. She clenched her fists and tried for a merry smile. She guessed by the look on Jack's face that she failed. At least with the flickering candle-light, it might be a little more difficult to see how shiny her eyes were, and how hard she was fighting tears.

As good as it was to have Jack back at the house, she knew that she'd have to describe what she'd experienced and that forced her to think over and over again about the body.

She should have thought better of getting Victor to sleep. If he'd been awake and rabid, she'd have been distracted from what she'd seen. The quiet dinner that had turned too often to what Violet had seen had made it impossible for her to relax. Only Jack's presence made her feel safe.

Why had someone killed a country gardener? Why would anyone do such things to another human being? It didn't matter that she'd been involved in more than one murder investigation, she still found the act of murder to be inexplicable.

"Violet, darling." Lila pressed a glass of ginger wine into Vi's hand moments after they entered the parlor. "I think you need this."

"The last time we pressed alcohol on her after seeing a body, she was nearly useless. I need to hear about what happened." Jack cleared his throat. "I do need the details of everything, Vi. Please."

"Ginger wine is Violet's comfort. She doesn't get zozzled on it. She sips it and calms down."

Jack's head cocked as he examined Violet. "How did I not know this?"

"Perhaps that penetrating, alert gaze of yours that seems to know all is just an act?" Denny poured himself a glass of ginger wine as he said, "Violet has made me love the stuff too. I also like ginger beer these days. It's her fault I'm addicted to chocolates too. I feel certain that must be true."

"Yes, that could only be my fault. I'm sure you had never had them before meeting me." She knew she was being waspish.

Denny winked at Violet and propped his feet up on an ottoman. "I certainly have no recollection of them before you. It must be so."

"Mmmm." Violet sipped her mind and ignored Denny's cheery nonsense. She had the impression it was merely to distract her, but she found it impossible to be distracted.

"You're a hard woman," Denny told Vi. "Lila would never drug me." He patted his wife's knee. "Unlike you—"

"Oh, laddie," Lila muttered, cutting him off. "You had better stuff it, darling."

Kate glanced among them all, shaking her head. "Are you never serious, Denny?"

"I was quite serious when I had to work. Pretending to work all of the time was exhausting. Reports that had to make sense but didn't have all the facts. I suppose they'd have sent me on my way before long, but my dear, sweet aunt saved me from slaving away."

The others laughed as Violet rose and crossed to the paintings on the wall. Her gaze settled on a familiar face. Aunt Agatha smirked down from the wall. Violet felt as though her aunt were sharing a joke with her. It had been, Violet remembered, Aunt Agatha who'd first put a little something in Victor's tea after he'd become ill and vicious.

Violet's eyes burned as she stared at her aunt, mother of her heart, mentor, and the first person Violet knew who had been murdered. It had been such a hard journey since Aunt Agatha had died. Even with meeting and falling in love with Jack, even with the addition of Kate to their family, even...

Someone set a soft hand on Violet's arm, and she glanced over to see Kate looking at Aunt Agatha as well. "I wish I could have known her."

"She'd have liked you." Violet felt a rush of pain at the realization that her beloved friend would never meet the woman who had raised and loved Violet and Victor. Someday, Violet would raise children and only be able to tell them stories of Agatha.

"Are you all right?" Kate asked gently, but when Violet turned to truly face her friend, she caught the concerned gazes of Jack, Lila, and Denny.

"No," Violet admitted.

"Tell us what happened," Jack said.

"You heard Victor...."

"We did," Kate agreed. "He deserved to have his ears boxed."

"What you didn't know was that I had asked Mrs. King about walks nearby. Once I decided to leave, I wanted to explore on my own. I didn't want to rehash how Vic was being awful. I didn't want to be commiserated with. I needed a break."

"You do—"

Lila elbowed Denny before he could finish his statement. No doubt it was something to the effect of how Violet set Victor off. She knew she did. She didn't take it when he lashed out at her, and she wasn't going to start. Not even if he was ill.

"I stopped in the graveyard. I knew the walk was behind it, but I wasn't quite sure where it started. I wasn't in a hurry. I did feel guilty about leaving you with my bicycle but decided that Victor deserved it."

Jack snorted.

"That he did." Lila patted Denny and added, "I am taking notes, darling husband. Violet is showing me the way of keeping you in line."

Violet ignored them, speaking directly to Jack though she paced as she did, fiddling with her bracelets. "Eventually, I started down the path. Picked a flower, said hello to a horse whose pasture linked up to the path. It was while I was saying hello to that fine fellow that we both heard something."

"He hadn't been dead long when I saw him," Jack said.

Violet shuddered, and Kate wrapped a comforting arm around Violet.

"Does that mean the killer might have been right there?" Lila gasped. Her gaze flit from Violet to Jack to Denny, and they all looked shaken.

"Possibly." Jack's voice was deep and rough as though he were holding back something intense.

"I didn't see anything," Violet told him. "I saw the body. Ran. Realized he could be alive, returned to check. When it was clear that it was too late, I ran for you."

"You did just right," Jack said. "Thank God that you were all right. If the killer had been there…"

They all shivered at the idea of the killer watching Violet stumble over the body. What if the killer had been on the other side of the body? What if she'd run the wrong way? Violet sniffed and Jack muttered, "I'm not sure I can ever let you go off on your own again."

Both Kate and Lila snorted at that, and Jack's ears turned red. Denny laughed straight out at his reaction as the girls mocked him.

"I'm fine," Violet told Jack.

"That remains to be seen." He took her hand when she paced by him again and pulled her down next to him. "You are, however, safe now. I'll help the locals find this killer, and it'll all be over."

"What did you find out, old man?" Denny asked as he rose to make cocktails, refilling his own glass of ginger wine as well as Violet's before making G&Ts for everyone else.

"I was officially called in and helped the local boys lay down the start of the case. Sent the body off with the coroner. Talked to anyone who might have seen something—no one did."

"Or no one will admit to it," Kate added.

Jack didn't disagree. "I went to tell the wife what had happened. She has a little cottage not far from here. She wasn't well."

"Wasn't well how?" Lila cut in this time. She glanced at Violet and then said, "I suppose you heard about how they lost four children on one day?"

"I hadn't heard that." Jack shook his head. "Mrs. Jones looked as though someone had roughed her over. I asked her who had done it, but she wouldn't say. Her brother came by while we were there. He'd heard rumors of his brother-in-law's death. The two of them didn't seem so friendly with each other."

"Mr. Freckleton?" Violet turned her bracelet on her wrist slowly, trying to imagine having been beaten and then finding out that you were a widow. If her husband had been the one who hurt her, was she relieved that he was dead? Perhaps not.

If her husband had not been the one who hurt her, who had? Could that person be the killer of Jones?

"Why would she protect whoever hurt her?" Lila sounded as baffled as Violet felt.

"Maybe it was her husband," Kate suggested. "If he hurt her and then was murdered, maybe she's afraid that someone will think it was her who killed him."

"How did he die?" Violet asked. "I…I…didn't look. I didn't want to see."

"He was stabbed." Jack took Violet's hand. "Don't imagine it. I know you have a vivid mind that can paint that picture, but don't do that to yourself."

Violet glanced around the parlor. The fire was crackling, and it was romantic with the burning candles lighting the room. Her friends were all staring her way as she paced again. She just might slip a little laudanum into her own wine and let it take her to sleep. She wasn't sure why Jack, who didn't have to work, got involved in investigation after investigation, but it wasn't something that Violet enjoyed.

"Was Mrs. Jones lovely?"

Jack paused before he answered. Long enough that Violet wasn't quite sure why he was waiting. She turned to face him and his sharp gaze was fixed on her as though he could read her thoughts.

"She was quite beautiful. Though too thin and very pale. Like a ghost of a beautiful woman, really."

"Mr. Freckleton seemed quite well-educated. He couldn't have been happy when his sister married a gardener."

"How do you know Freckleton?"

"I met him in the graveyard when I read the children's graves."

"Still mourning over dead children." Denny shook his head and set aside his wine. "Maybe Freckleton killed Jones due to something about those little ones."

Violet bit her lip and then shook her head. "They died years ago. If someone was going to get murdered over them, it would have happened then. We don't know how they died, either. It could have been a terrible accident."

"It's not a good thing that he was so nearby where Jones died surely?" Lila tucked her hair behind her ear and took Denny's hand, shivering at the idea of Violet chatting with a murderer.

"But certainly, I am his alibi," Violet said. "I had just seen him. Why would he kill his brother-in-law now? His sister had married low years before. She'd had and lost four children. If Jones was violent with his wife, surely that wasn't the first time. Mr. Freckleton might have reason to hate Jones, but don't you think he'd have killed the man long before?"

"We don't know why he died." Jack shoved his hands through his hair. "Until we find out why someone might have wanted to kill Jones, we can't make any conclusions. Violet makes a good point though. I'm far more concerned over the husbands of the women we saw him with. Or, the women themselves, if they really did have a relationship with him and perhaps were led to expect something from him."

Violet couldn't imagine any of it. That was the problem. In the end, as snobbish as it sounded, Philip Jones was a gardener. He took care of a house that had been mostly empty and was run down. As much as Vi hadn't liked him, she still asked herself: Why kill a gardener?

CHAPTER 11

*V*iolet had heard Jack leave the next morning. It wasn't that he was loud, but the person who'd come to pick him up had an auto that was downright rambunctious. Violet fancifully thought that it sounded a bit like a mechanical bear. The vehicle woke her enough to order some tea for Victor. She doctored a cup for him with additional laudanum, and then grabbed Denny as he went down to the breakfast room to deliver a second doctored cup when Victor inevitably rejected hers.

"I am not drinking that," Victor told Violet. His frown was ferocious, and Violet deliberately lifted a brow and pretended to have a sip of Victor's first cup of doctored tea.

"I'm just trying to help your throat," she lied with a fierce scowl. She called, "Denny! Give Victor your cup!"

Denny walked in, lowering the teacup from his mouth and examining Victor. "I suppose you can have this one, old boy."

On any other day, Victor would have caught the smirk on the corner of Denny's mouth and known that both cups were doctored, but he missed it entirely. After swallowing aspirin and the doctored tea, he fell back to sleep before even realizing he had been drugged once again.

"You're a good friend," Violet told Denny, patting him on the arm. "Enjoy your breakfast."

Violet went back to her bedroom and snuggled back into her bed. Victor might not willingly sleep the morning away, but Violet was not so particular. Her night had been interrupted with nightmares of dead bodies, of being chased through the wood, of ghosts of small children crying out for their father. Violet sniffed and curled into her pillows, forcing her mind to think of nothing but Cuba, ocean crossings, and dancing.

When she woke again, the sun had risen well into the sky. Beatrice had come and gone with Violet's dog, Rouge. No doubt the dog had been walked, played with, fed, and brushed. Violet assumed the creature was following Beatrice around.

Vi rose and dressed, trying to keep herself from thinking of the murder, but she wasn't able to. She had seen someone killed for their money. Violet's sister's fiancé had been killed out of jealousy. Violet knew a woman who had been killed for manipulating her lovers. There had even been a girl that Violet had met who had been killed because a man had been obsessed with her. She intended to leave their village, and it had cost her the remainder of her life.

She tried to keep her mind from the murder, thinking of Victor's house. She didn't like it. In fact, she hated it. She didn't like that it was so far from Jack. Any visit to Victor, if Violet married Jack, would have to be well thought-out. She couldn't imagine spending weeks apart from her twin, let alone months and months.

Violet sighed. Those thoughts weren't making her any happier. She had bathed and dressed, not thinking too much about what she wore for once. She glanced down, noted the grey and blue plaid dress with a drop waist and pleats and thought they'd go well with her sensible shoes.

The storm had ended but the lights were still out. She supposed that someone was working on getting things fixed for them. Violet wasn't concerned. The day had dawned bright and blue, and Violet decided that she wanted to go home to London.

That wasn't going to happen as long as Jack was investigating into this case. She could leave him and Victor, get on the train with her maid, and go home. She didn't want to do that either. She rubbed her hand over the back of her neck. If she wanted to get out of this house and not leave Jack and Victor behind, then the killer must be found.

Violet considered what she knew about what had happened to Philip Jones as she paced her bedroom. She grabbed her journal and pulled it out, looking over the lackadaisical notes that she'd made with Lila. Slowly, as if bending her will to the distasteful task, Violet seated herself at the desk in her bedroom, frowning down at the journal. She flipped to the blank pages at the back and wrote:

PHILIP JONES— murdered in the wood. Seen with two separate women—neither of whom had been his wife. His wife had been beaten. Had Philip committed that crime? Was it something to do with the house? Mrs. King guessed there might be something valuable inside. Perhaps when Philip was keeping an eye on the house, he'd stolen something? If so, maybe someone had realized?

Violet tapped her pen against her mouth, thinking of all the reasons people killed each other. Money, love, jealousy, hatred. Who had emotions that ran that deep about Philip Jones? As she asked herself the question, she was surprised that she had so many answers.

"Violet," she told herself, "you are a right snob."

The question of *why kill a gardener* was hitting her again, but this time she was forcing herself to answer. You killed him because you loved him, wanted something from him, or hated him. You killed him because there was more to the man than planting roses and trimming hedges. You killed him because you were a bad person, and he had placed himself on the wrong side of you. Maybe you killed him because he was a bad person, but in the end—he was murdered because he wasn't just a side character in Violet's life. He was, in fact, the protagonist of his own story as everyone was, regardless of their station.

Violet ended her scold. She titled the next section of her journal SUSPECTS.

MRS. JONES— Someone had given her a beating. Had it been her husband? If so, perhaps she'd finally had enough. Or had it been someone else? Maybe Jones had gone after the person who'd hurt his wife and lost?

Violet's mouth twisted. Mrs. Jones hadn't told Jack who had hurt her. Would she tell a woman? Perhaps a former employer who'd come with an offer to pay for the funeral or give her a good start? Violet guessed that Mrs. Jones needed help, and if she wasn't the killer, the right thing to do would be to visit her, give condolences, and offer support.

The next person Violet wrote was the friendly Mr. Freckleton.

JOSEPH FRECKLETON—He lost his niece and nephews in one tragedy and was still affected. What happened? If Jones had been the one who had hurt Freckleton's sister, maybe it was Freckleton who had finally reached his limits? Then again, why after all this time?

It didn't add up for Violet. Victor would murder a man for beating Violet. That being said, however, he was a particularly protective brother. After this many years of marriage, would Freckleton suddenly step in? Violet didn't see that either. She frowned down at her journal and left space for the questions that didn't have answers.

A part of her wanted to remove him from the list. Any man who mourned nieces and nephews and was so friendly to random strangers didn't strike Violet as a murderer. She supposed, however, that he had to be kept on if she were to be thorough.

Violet turned her thoughts from the brother and moved onto the next person. He seemed like a much likelier candidate to Vi.

JAMES BAKER— The man had discovered his wife right after an assignation. She had smoothed her looks out pretty well for what Violet had seen, but what if Mr. Baker knew his wife had been having an affair with Philip Jones?

Violet rather thought James Baker would have the same ingrained prejudices against a gardener that Violet had discovered she possessed. How would he feel that his seemingly respectable wife was conducting an affair in the wood? Violet suspected any man would be furious about his wife stepping out on him. Of course he would, but perhaps there was a special kind of rage when prejudices came into play?

Beatrice peeked into the bedroom and said, "Oh Lady Violet, I am happy to see you are up. Mrs. Lila and Miss Kate wanted to ensure you were all right when you didn't come down for breakfast."

"Feared I'd dove into a relapse? Perhaps I have swooned over the things I've seen. Yes, I'm all right, darling. I have just been working some things out in my mind."

Violet examined her maid. Beatrice, Violet suddenly realized, was someone you would kill over. Perhaps Vi's prejudice wasn't as ingrained as she'd thought. Perhaps it wasn't so much that Jones was a gardener but that she hadn't liked Jones. Or maybe Vi's prejudices were sneakier, bypassing the servants she cared for and focusing only on the ones she had no feelings over. Either way, she vowed to adjust her thinking.

"Perhaps, luv, you might bring me a tea tray and some toast and tell my friends I'll be down soon? I just want to finish this."

"Of course, my lady." Beatrice left the room, but Rouge took the chance to curl up at Violet's feet rather than follow the maid. Victor's dog was nowhere to be seen, but Violet guessed Gin was curled up with Victor, exulting in the fact that Victor was easily accessible. It was a feeling that Violet could identify with.

She scowled at her bedroom again, feeling as though it were a concrete example of their eventual separation, then went back to work. She wouldn't think on that now, even though she realized the house was nice—she hated it. She had been hoping that it would be terrible, and Victor would sell it and accept a loss.

Enough of that, Violet ordered herself. She added the next name that occurred to her to her journal.

MELODY BAKER — Jones's lover. Would she have killed him? Perhaps he was threatening her? Maybe she was trying to hide her affair from her husband and couldn't count on Jones's discretion?

Violet shut the journal. She wasn't sure who she'd seen in the street with Mr. Jones, but the woman had seemed all too familiar with him. Violet wasn't sure who else might want to kill him. She didn't know enough about the man to be able to easily identify all his potential enemies. Perhaps, however, Violet thought, she had an idea of who might know those things.

She crossed to her wardrobe and pulled out her coat. She laid it over the back of her bed and put on her sensible shoes. This was a conservative little village, so Violet left off the heavier makeup this time. She wanted the locals to work with her, not shun her.

Violet paused at her face and dabbed light powder over her freckles. She lightly blackened her lashes and put on a light colored lipstick that was a shade darker than her own lips. She still looked conservative but felt better about her overall appearance.

While Violet was waiting, she removed the bangle she'd put on that morning but added a ring to play with. It looked warm outside but wet. She knew too well how the wet could get into your bones, so she grabbed a scarf in case her ramble left her too cold.

Just as she was ready to go, Beatrice returned with the tea and toast. Violet picked up her toast as the maid started to straighten Violet's bedroom.

"I'm going for a walk, darling. Would you please check on my brother? And bring me the dogs and leashes. I'll take them with me."

Beatrice nodded and started to get Rouge ready while Violet ate and then peeked in on Victor and found him snoring. He was so loud, she knew he'd have a sore throat when he woke. She crossed to him and shoved on his shoulder until he rolled onto his side and his snoring stopped.

Violet found Victor's dog lying at the end of his bed and clucked to him. Gin looked at Violet and refused to move.

"Come on, boy," she told him.

He looked at her as if she were stupid and snuggled closer to Victor's legs.

"Come on now," she snapped.

He harrumphed and closed his eyes.

Violet stared at the dog and then grabbed his collar, pulling him out of the room.

"You," she told the creature, "are as spoiled and stubborn as your master."

He whined and dragged his feet, attempting to sit down, but Violet was not going to be beaten by a dog she could carry with one hand. Gin and Rouge only got exercise because the twins had servants who helped with the dogs, but Violet needed the dogs as an excuse to nose her way through the town. The dogs would be her disguise.

Violet took the leash from Beatrice, put it on Gin's collar and took Rouge's leash in her other hand. She hurried down the servant's staircase to the back door of the house. She wanted to slip away before her friends caught her. They were casual enough with each other that they'd entertain themselves without either Victor or Violet being present, so she didn't feel too bad about leaving them behind.

She wouldn't, however, put it past Jack to have told Kate and Denny to keep an eye on Violet. In fact, Violet admitted, she was betting he'd done just that. Lila, at least, could be counted on to laugh at Jack, solemnly swear to do his bidding, then determinedly forget his instructions.

Violet turned the collar up on her coat and started down the drive. The walk into the main part of the village wasn't so far she needed to take an auto. She had made it about halfway down the drive when Kate came running up behind her.

"Vi!"

Turning slowly, Violet examined the woman. "Jack?"

"I had to cross my finger over my heart when I promised to keep you out of trouble."

"Impossible!" Violet declared merrily, accepting her companion with a grin.

"Just what I said. Apparently Jack can tell when I lie to him. He made me promise, therefore, to not leave you alone to your shenanigans. He said and I quote, 'Fine then. I won't try to box in our Vi. Perhaps you'd just keep her company?'"

Violet grinned and winked at Kate. "Ready for trouble then?"

"Lead on, O Captain! My Captain!"

Vi tucked her arm through the crook of Kate's elbow and handed over Gin's leash as they hurried down the drive together. The dogs had stopped fighting the adventure, and Violet's mind was racing ahead to the people she hoped to find and the discussions she hoped to have.

CHAPTER 12

"What do you think of the house?" Kate watched a bird in the distance before glancing at Violet.

"It's better than I thought it would be." Violet's laugh was rather wooden and she could feel the weight of Kate's gaze searching her carefully averted face.

Violet didn't want to admit she felt it was too far from Jack's country home, so she avoided Kate's gaze. It felt ridiculously presumptive to declare that the house was despised simply because its location was too far from a man who hadn't proposed, hadn't said he loved her, and hadn't made any promises.

She'd felt certain before that Jack loved her, and perhaps if she were honest, she still thought he did. Yet, he had said nothing. Did all women feel so shaky in their romances or was it only Violet?

What was Kate thinking? Violet hoped that Kate knew of Victor's affections. Both knew of them and knew that she should let him down gently if she didn't return them. But no, of course Kate loved Victor. Otherwise she'd have returned home to the life she had overtly told them she liked.

"It really is quite beautiful here," Violet said to change the subject.

"I find I am missing the blue skies and warmth of Cuba, but there is something about home."

"I'd miss the rain if I lived somewhere so magical as Cuba." Kate sounded almost as if she were in a confessional. "I enjoy our weather. I know that many prefer to escape the greyness of England but not I."

"Do you not want to travel further?"

"Oh, I do." Kate smiled at Violet. "I just want to come home in between."

The wind picked up and sent Violet's short bob flying around her head. They were in the village main, and she was sure their progress was being tracked.

"The dogs were a clever ploy." Kate's attention was caught by a woman who had started out by frowning at them, then paused on the sight of the dogs. How could they be scandalous Londoners when they were simply two young women walking a set of small spaniels?

"I think we should temporarily rename the dogs Muffin and Rex." Violet smiled brightly at a couple of children and crossed to them. "Hello, my little darlings. Isn't it a fine day?"

One of the grubby-faced little girls squeaked, tossed her braids over her head and went pelting away.

"Well now." Kate put her hands on her hips. "What an odd greeting." She grinned and winked at the remaining children while Violet eyed the group.

She looked for a mischievous gaze, found one, and met it in open challenge. The scamp was just what she needed. He looked as though he had a frog in his pockets with that twinkle in his eyes. He was a ginger with freckles and a few pieces of hair that stuck straight up. She bet his mother bemoaned those hairs. He was wearing clothes that been cleaned and pressed at one point, but the dirt on his face said he'd been up to mischief already.

"Hello there," Vi said to the mischievous one. "You look a likely lad."

"Likely enough," he declared with a half-smirk. The challenge remained in his gaze and when Violet lifted a brow at him, he echoed her movement. She couldn't help but grin at that.

She held out her hand, and he shook it. She suspected if she stayed here very much, she'd become fast friends with this little man. "Do you know Mrs. King?"

"Mebbe."

Kate snorted, choking back a laugh.

"I'm guessing that answer is dependent upon a sixpence?" Violet mused.

The boy's eyes widened and he nodded frantically. "Yes, mum."

"Lead the way, my lad."

The boy darted ahead, skipping forward and then bouncing on his toes as he waited for Kate and Violet to catch up.

"Looking for local gossip?" Kate asked as they followed the lad.

Violet glanced sideways at Kate and explained her reasoning. "Mrs. King caught us in a train station, while I was clearly ill, and still took her chance to find out what she could about us. I'd eat my cloche if I thought she hadn't shared it at her next knitting circle or ladies' meeting. If any woman is going to know the dirty details of Philip Jones's life *and* tell us, it is Agnes King."

"Or his wife," Kate suggested.

Violet glanced back before nodding. "I'm saving her for later. I don't want to arrive too early to visit her. But, regardless of her answers, she needs help from Victor, I think."

Kate paused. Not because she disagreed, but because many an employer who had just hired someone wouldn't be stepping in to help the family. Philip Jones may have worked in the garden of Higgins House for quite some time, but Victor had only owned it for a short while.

When you added in that Jones had been late from the first day, the reason why they hadn't been able to hire local servants, and caught having an assignation during work hours—it was a sheer act of pure charity to help his wife out.

And yet, Victor and Violet had been raised by a woman who was both generous and practical. Getting someone on their feet was something Aunt Agatha would do. She might expect whomever she helped to stand on their own after that, but she would have given them a hand up. Violet would never do anything less than what she thought her aunt would have them do.

The walk to Agnes King's home wasn't too long even though the child kept trying to hurry them.

"In a race for your sixpence?" she asked.

The boy held out a grubby palm, and Violet put the coin in his hand, looking to Mrs. King's house. It was a respectable house but nothing that proclaimed wealth—a respectable cottage with a lovely garden. Violet's favorite part of it was the two brick pillars that framed the path that led to the front door. The pillars were topped with stone statues of house cats. The irony in the stonework made Violet chuckle.

Mrs. King had a bench under an oak tree, and she was sitting on it.

"What's all this?"

"We're invading you," Violet said. "We've been walking the dogs and taking in the sights and wondered if you could give me some advice."

"Advice?" Mrs. King sounded skeptical, and she should. Violet didn't need advice, she was simply using the chance to ask about helping Mrs. Jones as an avenue to get the local gossip. Regardless of what Mrs. King said, Violet was going to do what she could for the widow.

"Well, I fear it's a rather delicate matter." Violet glanced around and Mrs. King stood, taking a chair from near her door and crossing back to the bench.

"Perhaps I can offer you some tea?"

"That would be lovely." Kate smiled winningly. "What are these purple flowers called?"

Violet listened to Kate chat with Mrs. King while she rang the bell for her servant to request a tea tray. Kate smoothly inquired after Mrs. King's family, discovering her children were grown and she had three grandchildren. While they talked, Violet pasted an attentive expression on her face even though she wasn't paying much attention.

When the tea arrived, Mrs. King poured them all a cup. Once they were leaning back with their tea, Violet said, "I'm sure you've heard of the unfortunate loss of Mr. Philip Jones?"

"I heard of his murder," Mrs. King replied. "I've also heard that one of your friends is involved in the investigation. To be honest, I'd have thought that a couple of earl's children wouldn't be larking about with bobbies even if your friend is a chief inspector or whatever such nonsense they use to refer to him."

"Those titles," Violet said brightly, as though she wasn't bothered by how the woman referred to Jack, "refer to their skill and experience. Mr. Wakefield is quite a brilliant investigator. I'm sure he'll have this case wrapped up even though *who would kill a gardener?*"

Even though she'd scolded herself quite thoroughly earlier that day, Violet used the same presumptions she'd despised herself for quite on purpose.

"Yes, well," Mrs. King's lips pursed and then she said, "he wasn't the most ordinary of gardeners."

"Oh?" Kate sipped her tea with her spine ramrod straight, turning her bright, clever eyes on Mrs. King. The woman clearly favored Kate over Violet and her friend was using the feeling to their advantage.

"He did marry quite beyond his class. His poor wife. She gave up everything for him and then he spent the next decade and a half moving among any woman who'd give him the time of day. I told Mrs. Jones she should take advantage of the new marriage act. If any woman deserved to escape the life she created, it was Mrs. Jones. I suppose someone else freed her instead."

"They had children, I saw. I found the poor little mites' graves… what a terrible tragedy."

"Oh yes, the children. They are why I pushed Mrs. Jones into divorcing her husband. Normally I wouldn't endorse such a scandalous action. Who God has put together and what not…"

Violet and Kate glanced at each other, and Vi guessed her own expression was as alarmed as Kate's. "What happened to the children?" Kate's voice was a hoarse whisper.

Mrs. King's pursed mouth flattened into an angry line. "Indeed. It was terrible. Even after all this time, I can't help but feel heartbroken over it. Truthfully, poor Meredith has never been the same. And who can blame her?"

Violet glanced at Kate, who carefully asked, "But what happened to the children?"

"Well, Mr. Freckleton—that's Meredith's brother. He was married at the time. Married a sickly little thing and they hadn't been blessed with children. Only she was expecting. Rather far along and feeling quite poorly. Mr. Freckleton asked his sister for help. She'd had four children and knew what to expect. So, Meredith got her children to bed, left them tucked up tight. Mr. Jones was there if they needed anything. They mostly looked after themselves when their mama wasn't around. Even the little girl. A little angel, she was."

Violet bit her lip. The shock of pain didn't help. Her fingers were digging into her palms. Little Rouge seemed to sense Violet's feelings and placed a paw on Violet's foot. It didn't help. Nothing was going to better the end of this tale because it ended with four graves and four deaths on the very same day.

"That cad Jones left the children. There must have been a spark or something. The cottage caught fire. Maybe he left something too near the fireplace? Maybe one of the little ones got up and caused an accident? Whatever happened, those babies died in a house fire. All on one day. If that weren't bad enough, Mr. Jones was seen out with one of the local loose girls. He'd left the children to step out on his wife and all while she was helping others."

"Oh my heavens," Kate said.

Violet didn't say anything. She couldn't find the words. Her fingernails were digging into her palms and the pain demanded she loosen her grip on her own hands, but she couldn't. Violet hadn't wanted children, not really. Not before meeting and falling in love with Jack, anyway. Even still, she couldn't help but put herself in Mrs. Jones's shoes. To have them and lose them—Violet didn't see things getting better after that.

Of course the woman had to have been head over heels in love, swept off her feet in love to marry a gardener when she could have had an easier life. She had fallen in love and right out of the life she was accustomed to. It was a right she had—to marry whomever she chose! Violet wouldn't take that from her. Never.

But Mr. Jones! That cad hadn't honored what his wife had done. Hadn't appreciated her. He'd stepped out on her and left her heartbroken. As if that wasn't enough, his philandering had cost them their children.

"I suppose," Kate said softly, "we can never know if his not being there saved his life or cost the children theirs."

"Just what the vicar said." Mrs. King didn't sound convinced. "That being true, I can't say I didn't wish he'd died with them than to leave his poor wife wondering. It would have been a mercy to lose him rather than have him live and wonder."

Violet did not disagree. Not at all. Kate didn't seem quite so heartless as the other two women, and they united in their feelings. Violet nodded at Mrs. King who gave her enough of a smile to make Violet feel as though she'd finally shaken whatever it was that Mrs. King didn't like about Violet.

"What happened to Mrs. Freckleton?" Kate cleared her throat and set down her teacup with shaking hands.

"She didn't survive childbirth. Mr. Freckleton and his sister lost everyone but each other in only a few months. I don't include Mr. Jones, of course."

"Of course." Violet sipped her tea and considered. "I suppose Jack must be trying to track down all of Mr. Jones's lovers to determine whether they or possibly their spouses were the killer."

"You don't think Mr. Freckleton killed his brother-in-law?" Kate asked, surprised.

Violet shrugged. "He struck me as a gentle man when I met him in the graveyard. Still putting flowers on the graves of those children."

"Hmmm," Mrs. King mused.

"Is he not gentle?" Kate asked. "We could hardly know. A few minutes over the graves of children is hardly the place to determine the nature of a person."

Mrs. King did not answer the question. Instead she turned to Violet and asked, "What advice do you need?"

"I was wondering what I should do to help Mrs. Jones in the loss of her husband."

Mrs. King's already straight spine seemed to lengthen as she considered. Her teacup was balanced precisely on her knee and there was nary a wobble in the tea. Violet watched with more admiration than such a skill probably deserved but all the same, Violet was in awe.

"Is your brother inclined to generosity? I wouldn't have thought it."

Violet barely kept her eyes from narrowing coldly on the woman.

"He did buy a home in a rather spectacular way. Mr. Carlyle is, however, quite kind," Kate answered before Violet could. The firmness in Kate's tone had Mrs. King lifting a brow, but she didn't argue.

"I can't imagine that Mrs. Jones could easily pay for a funeral. Though I think it likely that her brother will give her a home if she needs one. I am not entirely sure what she has. She received her current home from her aunt. It has never been clear if there was money to go with it."

Violet nodded. "Would I talk to the vicar about easing that burden?"

"Yes, I think so."

CHAPTER 13

"Of all the…of all the nerve! Victor will never be anything other than a drunk in this village even after helping the poor widow."

Violet noted Kate's fury was directed at the reception of Victor rather than at the death of the children. Violet shuddered as she thought of that again. To lose so deeply. It was awful. Victor's lot was the result of his actions. He should have known better to get so zozzled that he ended up buying a house. Especially one that he hadn't seen and would not have otherwise bought—at least Violet hoped he wouldn't have.

Violet tried to smile at Kate, but Vi wasn't up to it. Maybe it was the walk after a restless night of sleep and being ill for days. She scoffed at herself. Her melancholy was for the house. Perhaps she should work on improving her heart. She should be happy for her brother that he hadn't been taken advantage of more than he had been.

The vicar was easy enough to find. He had a little house near the church. There was a young woman crying into a handkerchief in the garden. Violet and Kate saw her and then pretended to completely miss her as they approached the door. Violet, however, considered the timing of the girl's tears even as she and Kate smoothed their faces into perfect politeness and knocked on the door.

It was opened a moment after by a uniformed maid who saw them inside. Violet told the dogs to lie down. Victor and Violet weren't responsible for how well-behaved they were, but Violet had no worries that they'd remain where they were. The vicar was in his office, but they were left in a parlor while the housekeeper inquired if he could receive them.

"What do you think the girl was crying about?" Kate asked.

Vi shook her head. Her answer was so low Kate had to lean forward to hear it, but Violet didn't want to be caught talking about some poor girl who was trying to have a good cry. "You were that young once. For a bit there, I was crying for no reason at all. Victor or Father looked at me wrong and I was squalling into my pillow, telling myself the most woeful stories. I almost liked it. That being said, someone died yesterday, and I'd bet half the kingdom that her tears have to do with it. Otherwise, why would she be hiding in the garden?"

Kate's gaze widened, and she nodded in agreement.

Then she was unable to hold back a laugh. "I can hardly imagine you crying and bemoaning. Victor must have hated that so much."

"He used to curse at me and stomp away. I always wailed a little louder after he did. It only spurred him on. You could hear the echoes of his curses as he fled."

Kate's shout of laughter escaped as the parlor door opened and the vicar entered the room. He crossed to them as Kate tried to muffle her giggles.

"Hullo!" Vi said brightly. She remembered a moment later why they were there and added, "I am Violet Carlyle. I have come on behalf of my brother, Victor Carlyle, who is ill and has sent me in his stead."

"I am Father George Bosch." He held out his hand and greeted both of them while Violet introduced Kate.

"Your brother is the one who bought the Higgins house? I have been intending to come visit you, but I did hear from the doctor that you've been ill. My apologies for my tardiness."

"Think nothing of it." Violet waved off his apology. "I've actually come to speak with you about poor Philip Jones. My brother would like to pay for his funeral and help Mrs. Jones. I was hoping you could help us facilitate the funeral portion of things?"

The vicar's brows rose and he nodded. "Oh, that is generous. It would be helpful and such a relief. That family has been so burdened. Mrs. Jones and Mr. Freckleton's parents with the influenza. Then the children, then Mrs. Freckleton. They lost two brothers in the war, and I fear there was some division between Mrs. Jones and her family before they passed."

Violet didn't have to pretend to a commiserating face. She was dying inside a little bit for poor Meredith Jones.

"What else can be done for her?"

The vicar made several suggestions and Violet nodded while Kate took notes. They left him in charge of telling whomever was hired by Mrs. Jones to send their bills to the Higgins house. Violet didn't even argue the name of the house. She hoped it would always be the Higgins house and Victor would unload it to the next drunk fool to pass through the village.

She and Kate left the house after getting directions to Mrs. Jones's home. The vicar had vaguely attempted to dissuade them from visiting Mrs. Jones. The way he spoke had made it clear to Violet he knew that Mrs. Jones had been beaten. Violet was deliberately dim until the vicar gave up.

Vi clucked for the dogs, gave both of the small spaniels a quick scratch, and picked up the dog leashes.

"He must have thought that we'll get turned away at the door," Kate said. "That made me so uncomfortable that it was hard for me to sit still. The vicar must also have thought you were quite the stupidest woman he's ever met."

Violet laughed. They turned the corner on the path out of the vicar's property and ran directly into the girl who had been crying before. He face was red and swollen. "Oh!"

"Oh, dear me." Violet caught the girl, who had jumped back and wobbled. "Terribly clumsy of me. My apologies."

The girl tried to escape, but Violet didn't let her go.

"Oh!" she said again. She blinked rapidly and twisted a little, but Violet took the girl's hand and squeezed, pretending to steady her even though she'd caught her balance and was trying to avoid eye contact.

"I *am* sorry. I fear this is the most terrible introduction. We've just come to visit, you see. Are you the vicar's daughter?"

The girl's manners came into play even though Violet was ignoring her own. "Ye—yes."

"I am Lady Violet Carlyle. This is my good friend, Kate Lancaster."

"I—I'm pleased to meet you." She sniffed and attempted to gather her emotions. "I'm Marie Bosch."

"I was wondering, Miss Bosch, if Kate and I might beg you for assistance. We're quite turned around, I'm afraid."

The girl nodded slowly. Violet was channeling her stepmother's imperious nature, imposing her will as a member of the peerage so the girl would bend to her. Kate's expression was shocked at Violet's behavior. Vi was shocked at herself, to be honest.

Marie led the way to Mrs. Jones's house with eyes that were becoming more and more frantic. Little sniffles escaped the girl, and Violet demanded, "Have things gone astray with your beau?"

Poor Marie jumped and a tear slipped down her cheek. The girl, Violet felt certain, was crying over Philip Jones. Vi had hoped she could use the girl's emotional state for a gossip on the journey to the widow's house.

Violet stopped and took the girl's hand. "You'll get through this, darling. There is no way that Mr. Philip Jones was a good choice for you."

Kate's squeak was hidden by Marie's gasp. Her eyes were wide and panicked. "How did you know?"

"I'm spoiled and frivolous, but unlike the general assumption, I am not stupid. You were crying, you're young, and you're panicking as we get closer to his wife."

"Oh, his wife!" Marie almost snarled.

Violet and Kate glanced at each other.

"Tell us about her, would you?" Kate asked gently.

"She blames him for their children dying. Made him the villain *for the whole village*. People hate him now. Hated him—" Marie sniffled into her handkerchief before continuing. "As though he didn't lose the children too, as though he isn't haunted by what-ifs. As though he wasn't blessed to avoid joining them in death. It's not his fault that they died. It's a miracle that he lived!"

Violet felt a flash of rage as she realized what Jones had done to this girl. Using her naiveté to make himself the victim. To make her want to love him and be the one who sees him truly while everyone else was too blind to see.

Kate was biting her bottom lip to hide her reaction to what Jones had done to Marie.

"So…" Kate said carefully. "I'm sorry…perhaps I am struggling with this whole brainwork thing. Let me clarify. Mrs. Jones left her children with her husband in order to help an ill woman, and Mrs. Jones is the villain."

"It was a tragedy! An act of God. Nothing more. But she turned poor Philip into the slayer of his own children instead of another mourning parent."

Violet swallowed in order to gather her thoughts. She was scrambling for something to say and coming up dry.

"We're sorry for your loss," Kate told Marie gently. "I am sure it's so much the worse when no one can understand what you're going through."

Violet's gaze widened at Kate's brilliance.

"Thank you for trusting us with your burden."

The girl wept a little more and Kate wrapped her arm around her shoulders, handing over a fresh handkerchief. They had reached the cottage under the trees where Mrs. Jones lived. The gate was closed and to Violet's surprise, the garden was a mess. The grass was too long, the flower beds were a riot of weeds, and the hedges were spiky and overgrown.

The house was also nicer and larger than anything a gardener could afford on his own, though it was small and cramped to Violet's standards. This must be the place that Mrs. Jones inherited from her aunt. It was certainly a nice little place, aside from the garden.

Marie scowled towards the house and muttered, "I have to go." She escaped before Violet could stop her.

Kate's and Violet's gazes met and Kate said, "I could kill him myself, I think."

"Do you think he persuaded her to anything other than a few kisses?"

The two women stared after the running girl.

"I really have no idea," Kate answered. "It's possible. I hate to say it's possible, but it is—"

"Someone would kill over that," Violet told Kate.

"The vicar?"

"Anyone who loves that girl would kill over that type of crime." Violet's frown was deep and intense, and it almost made her face hurt. "I knew I didn't like him."

"It's unfortunate that Victor chose the gardener over other local servants. It'll put more distance between him and them."

"He couldn't have known," Violet said. "But I agree. It doesn't matter. He'll never be anything more than the drunk fellow who bought a house sight unseen. The loose Londoner who lives a life of endless parties, cocktails, and jazz or whatever else it is that these people hate."

"You don't sound like you like it here."

Violet didn't answer. She opened the gate and headed towards the house. Yet again, she'd be setting aside her manners to see what she could find out, but she was absolutely determined. Violet wanted to go back to London. She hadn't enjoyed nearly any part of this trip, and she didn't like the idea of long weeks here. If things were resolved, she could make up a reason to go home and leave Victor to his home.

Maybe Violet should consider tracking down Isolde and Gerald. They'd left Monaco for Iceland. The twins' brother and sister had read some article about the northern lights and decided to go see them. Their letters were paintings with words about how beautiful it was.

Violet gave Kate a smile, but Vi wasn't convinced that she hadn't given her feelings away. Kate was too observant to get away with hiding much from her. She was also, however, much kinder and far more polite than Violet. Kate might let Vi have her secret feelings when Vi couldn't be counted on to do the same.

The cottage was a nice place for what it was. She was self-aware enough to know she was spoiled and that her life of living in mansions changed her outlook. But—for a gardener—it was quite nice. Larger than most would have with a snug little setup. Violet could see being happy in this place if you were in love. She bet that something along those lines was what the young Meredith Freckleton imagined.

If Jack were a gardener, Violet wouldn't even hesitate to join him in this house. Though Jack might want to second-guess such a thing, as Violet's practical household skills were almost non-existent.

Poor Mrs. Jones, she must have been head over heels like the young Marie, persuaded to believe in a happily-ever-after with the man of her heart and had it all snatched away when he ended up being a philandering scoundrel.

Approaching the woman, knowing it would further burden her, made Violet despise herself. Even still, she lifted her hand and knocked firmly and precisely.

CHAPTER 14

The woman who opened the door was older, uniformed, and clearly did not belong in the small cottage where Violet was intending to bully her way in.

"We're not at home," the woman said, starting to close the door before she'd even finished her sentence. Violet was certain that this woman did not work for the gardener. Who had lent Mrs. Jones a housekeeper? Violet was betting it had been Mr. Freckleton.

"My name is Lady Violet Carlyle," Vi responded snobbishly. "I am here representing my brother, Victor Carlyle, who—I'm sure you're aware—employed Mr. Jones. We come with an offer of assistance."

The woman paused, and Violet could see the offer of help fighting with what were no doubt strict instructions to turn everyone away. "One moment."

The door was shut in Violet's face. She glanced to Kate.

"We're bad people," Kate said, "intruding on the poor woman like this. Even if we are paying for the funeral."

"I know." Violet took Kate's hand and squeezed as the door opened. They'd already told the dogs to lie down, and both of them snuffled a little when Kate and Violet were led into the small front room. Violet took a seat at the housekeeper's direction with Kate squeezed onto the small seat next to her.

Could the housekeeper belong to Meredith Jones? That seemed unlikely. Violet considered for a moment and then bet herself that the woman normally worked for Mr. Freckleton.

The two of them glanced at each other. The room was empty and there was no sign of the widow. Violet pressed her mouth closed. The cottage was too small to get away with whispering about the murder, and Violet did not want to be caught being heartless.

Violet crossed her fingers in her lap. They were digging into the back of her hands, but it gave her a little balance against what she was doing. She took in a deep breath as the widow moved into the room. The housekeeper placed a pillow on the seat for the woman, and she moved like she was brittle. Violet wanted to search Mrs. Jones face, to read her expressions as they spoke, to hold out her hand and somehow bond with her. Meredith Jones was, however, wearing a black net veil over her face.

Violet blinked at the sheer shock of seeing a gardener's wife wearing something like that. Her dress was nicer than Violet would have expected. Though, now that she thought about it, Mr. Jones did have nicer clothes than the typical gardener. His pants weren't so worn, his shoes were of finer quality. She hadn't thought much of it at the time, but the dress Mrs. Jones was wearing had been carefully made.

Could she, Vi wondered, make her own clothes? Many women did who couldn't afford to buy clothes as Violet did, so they could be better dressed by simply making their own.

"Hello . . ." Mrs. Jones let her voice trail off.

Violet nibbled at her lip before she decided to be overly familiar. "Hello." Violet reached out her hand and took Mrs. Jones'. She stifled a whimper as Violet took hold, and Vi realized Mrs. Jones wasn't hiding her face because of the tears. It was the beating. Violet gently cradled the woman's hand.

"I have come to tell you that my brother, Victor, will be paying for your husband's funeral."

"Oh, my lady!" Mrs. Jones didn't object, and her voice shook with the reaction.

"Victor would also like to give you a little something to help you get started without your husband." Violet wanted to question the woman further to find out more. It wasn't going to happen though. She was going to leave this woman be for the moment. "We'll send over a care basket with some goods. We wanted to extend our condolences and let you know that you aren't alone. If you need additional assistance, we'd like to help."

"Why?" Mrs. Jones sounded baffled. "I won't pretend not to need your help, my lady. It's most appreciated, but I don't understand why your brother would be so generous with a man who barely worked for him. Philip was no long-employed retainer leaving behind a houseful of children." Her voice cracked on that last comment, and Violet pretended not to notice the widow's grief.

Instead, she admitted, "You are quite right. Mr. Jones wasn't a long time employee and it would perhaps be understood if we left you to your lot."

"It would," Mrs. Jones said.

"But we aren't going to do that. We might be believed to be frivolous good-for-nothings, but I would like to think there is a little something to redeem us."

Mrs. Jones's hand was shaking, and Violet wished she could somehow say something to make her burden easier. What was there to say? Perhaps this was a woman who accepted that her husband was a philanderer and still loved him. Perhaps this was the final loss that would break her. Perhaps she was already broken and didn't have it in herself to care. Perhaps she was relieved at his loss and unable to deal with the effect of those feelings.

"Is there anything else we can do?"

Mrs. Jones said no, so the purpose of the visit was over, at least for the time being. Violet and Kate left, allowing the poor woman to return to her bed.

"She's in a great deal of pain." Kate sounded as sick about it as Violet felt.

"She is." Violet licked her lips. Her hands were shaking, and the realization that someone had beaten that woman and *then* she'd lost her husband—it was more than Violet could imagine. "I can't decide if it's only physical or if she's mourning her husband as well. We should send a doctor to her."

"We should. And, her husband did seem like a snake in the bosom." Kate let her fingers trail over the picket fence as they walked away. Flowers were starting to bloom at the base of the fence and beyond the Jones's house, and the rest of the fences in the line of cottages were painted and cared for. "Still, he was her snake in the bosom."

"Let's go back to the house." Violet looked towards Higgins house. She refused to think of it as Victor's. "I could use a large cuppa and perhaps something to eat."

They walked towards the house for a few minutes, letting the dogs range in the field near the road when an auto pulled up alongside them. Jack got out of the vehicle, tapped the top of it, and the driver moved on. He met their gazes, lingering on Violet before holding out an arm to both of them, while they walked on together.

Luncheon had long since passed, and Violet felt terrible. She was tired and she didn't much like the way she'd behaved that day. Her head was hurting, and the sun was too bright in the sky even though the renewed chill and the snap of the wind proclaimed another spring storm was on its way.

"Were you able to keep her out of trouble?" Jack asked Kate as he tucked her hand through his second arm. They continued with each lady on an arm as they strolled towards Victor's house.

Kate's mocking laugh was all the answer he got.

"Did you find the killer?" Violet asked.

"Not yet, I'm afraid. We're pursuing several avenues, but there's no reason to believe any one is more likely than the other."

"No details for us?" Kate asked lightly, and Jack was the one who laughed mockingly. In previous investigations, they'd been able to draw information from him. The last had ended, however, with Violet hurt. Since then Jack's instincts were to wrap her up in wool and set her on a shelf. That she didn't let him was a nearly endless source of frustration.

"Were they able to get the lights back on?" he asked, rather than answering Kate.

"We left before it was done, if they were successful." Kate was the one who answered as Violet stared into the distance, thinking over the day.

Violet leaned into Jack's side. She had a bad taste in her mouth, and it wasn't just from her behavior. There was the painful way that Mrs. Jones moved and the sound of the young Marie taking Philip's part. Maybe there was something to the theory about the unfair blame that had been laid at Philip's feet. The truth was no one could say for sure if the children would have survived if he had been there. It could, however, be said rather clearly that he hadn't been there. If the children had been sleeping, well—that didn't mean that Philip would have been sleeping. Being there and awake would certainly have saved at least some of the children.

The murmur of Jack's voice cut into Violet's thoughts, and it took a second to realize that he was repetitively saying her name.

"Oh, yes?"

He grinned down at her, frowning a moment later. "You look pale."

"Realizing how awful people are will do that to you."

"What did you find out?"

"What did you find out?" she echoed.

Jack shook his head a little bit, but there was enough of a smile about his lips to tell her that he wasn't all that bothered by her hijinks. Though to be fair, very little about the day felt actually boisterous or fun.

"I should like to partake of some actual hijinks," she said.

Both Jack and Kate stared at Violet, and it took her a second to realize she was talking to herself aloud.

Violet giggled at the look on their faces. "It's just...I felt like I intended to be engaged in a sort of hijinks today. The idea of meeting the locals and sleuthing seemed sort of fun when we left the house."

Kate lifted a solitary brow. "Today was not fun."

"Exactly," Violet nodded. "Hijinks are fun and frivolous. Today left me sad for humanity. I find John Donne running through my head."

"Donne?" Jack asked.

"Not the poetry. That sermon. You know the one. I memorized it once. Ah...let me see. 'No man is an island, entire of itself; every man is a piece of the continent, a part of the main. If a clod be washed away by the sea, Europe is the less...any man's death diminishes me, because I am involved in mankind, and therefore never send to know for whom the bells tolls; it tolls for thee.'"

"What are you trying to say?" Kate asked, cocking her head and tucking her loose hair behind her ear.

"She's saying that the loss of even such a man as Philip Jones has left us the lesser." Jack's gaze had softened on Violet. "He was hardly the best example of mankind, Vi. Thinking that we have lost so very much is generous."

"True, I suppose." Violet wasn't convinced.

It wasn't that Jones was wonderful. She very much despised him. It wasn't that she mourned him so much as she mourned what he could have been. She mourned for the man who had entangled himself in so many lives. The lives of the young Marie, of Joseph Freckleton, of Mrs. Jones—they were the lesser despite Philip Jones's nature. They had lost something. Something not all that positive, it was true. But they had lost a vital, lively piece of their lives. She didn't know how to explain, so she shrugged and glanced back to the rolling fields they were passing.

Rouge was chasing Gin through the field, but he bounded around back at her. She leaned back from him, tail-wagging, and then barked furiously before leaping forward and racing ahead.

"That you find something to mourn in Jones is one of the things that I love about you."

Jack's steady voice normally steadied her, but she almost tripped at the word 'love.' He'd never officially said he loved her. That wasn't even a statement of love, not really. Violet could say something similar about Kate.

As hard as her heart beat to hear it, it wasn't quite what she longed to hear. And it didn't drive away the melancholy of her question. Was there really a loss in the death of a man like Philip Jones?

"If Marie Bosch were my daughter," Violet started, "Or even one of my little protégés, I would probably have considered murdering him myself. There are too many people who had a reason to kill Philip Jones. And yet, I think that if he had been all he could have been—if he had been true to the promises he had to have made to his wife—if he had used his power over the young Marie to turn her mind to things beyond his woeful state, well, he could have been a great man. That is what I mourn about him, what he could have been. I feel very melancholy, I suppose. My outlook is grim since I've been ill. I can't quite shake it."

"Murder will do that to you, Vi. Look on the bright side, love. There is so much to see that is good. People like Kate, like *you*, like Victor when he isn't being a blackguard of a brother."

Violet forced a laugh. "I suppose if I give up on mankind, I will always have my sweet Rouge."

The dog barked once at her name and then went back to sniffing the flowers.

"There is more to you than cocktails, jazz, and face powder," Kate told Violet. "Even if this town does not see beyond your surface. There's no need to be grim. We'll discover this murderer and be back to normal. Don't let the way these people have been treating us push you to being blue."

Jack frowned. Perhaps he hadn't caught the way people looked at them. He had spent most of his time out and about as a Scotland Yard man more than the sister of the person who bought a house drunk. Rather a large difference, really.

CHAPTER 15

"*M*y lady," Jack said as Violet left her room before dinner. "I believe you've asked for hijinks."

Violet stopped. She glanced around, noting the lights were on and the house seemed to be running smoothly despite Victor being bedbound and both Violet and Kate having left for the day. Violet had intended to go check on Victor before dinner, but Jack was blocking the door with a twinkle in his gaze. He had dressed in dinner attire. Not regular dinner attire, but what must have been his nicest suit. She blinked up at him with his pretty outfit and felt a flash of heat as she took in his grin.

Jack was not one of those smoothly handsome men. He was too large for that with a too-sharp gaze and an aura that declared he was taking note of everything that was happening.

Despite his rugged face, Violet wasn't sure that she'd ever found anyone more attractive. She enjoyed his massive size and how he made her feel small. He made her feel dainty. She loved the way his intelligence focused on her. The way that when everyone else saw yet another bright young thing, he saw *her*. The part of her that was intelligent, the part of her that was frivolous, the part of her that was loving, and even the hateful pieces of her. He saw all of her and still seemed to find her worth wanting. That might be the most intoxicating feeling she'd ever felt.

Jack lifted her hand to his mouth and pressed a kiss on the tip of her first two fingers.

"Hullo." She tried for cheery but wasn't sure she pulled it off.

"Your brother is fine," Jack said. "I gave him the option of staying in bed on his own or pouring more laudanum down his throat. He took the first option. His fever is broken, his man got him to eat. Given the yawning I witnessed, he'll be sliding back into sleep before long."

Violet laughed, relieved. She placed her hand on his arm, feeling a little underdressed. She'd chosen the first dress in her closet. It was navy blue with beading and a drop waist. It was by no means a dress she didn't like, but she hadn't put any effort into her wardrobe that evening.

Violet glanced up at Jack. "Hijinks?"

"Carousing even. Perhaps a bit of boisterous nonsense."

Violet laughed, the last traces of her mood fading as Jack winked at her. He led her down to the parlor where Denny had made drinks.

"Just a G&T, I'm afraid. I don't have Victor's brilliance."

"I'm not sure I'd use the word brilliance." Violet's barb made Denny snort as he pressed a drink into her hand.

"You need this, my friend. Your venom is showing."

Violet pretended to gasp.

She joined Jack on the chesterfield as she sipped her cocktail. "What's this promise of nonsense?"

"It's for after dinner." Jack had selected a brandy rather than a cocktail, and he sipped it with relish. Why did he need that drink? Brandy was like ginger wine for him. The drink he wanted when things had been rough.

Vi glanced him over. He was tense at the corner of his eyes and mouth. Had things been rough for Jack while working or had something else happened? Violet wanted to invite him to pour his problems into her lap, but she knew he wouldn't when he was worried about her.

It was the naps that kept him on high alert, she thought. It wasn't that she never napped before she got ill, but she suspected that the frequency and length of them had him eyeing her like an infant instead of a grown woman who was shaking off the last of her illness.

Before she could inquire further and before either of them were halfway through their drinks, the dinner gong rang. The dinner was one of the simpler meals they had. Roasted chicken and veg. The cook was adequate but not brilliant.

"Tell us what you learned, laddie?" Denny refilled his plate while Violet pushed her own away. They all turned to Jack, who shrugged. He considered, and Violet felt his gaze on her face, but she deliberately sipped her wine to avoid pressuring him with her wants.

"Not much, I'm afraid. Jones didn't have excessive debts. He wasn't well-liked. We didn't find any witnesses. I still cannot get the wife to tell me who hurt her. I can't be sure if she's protecting his memory or someone else. It was a very frustrating day, to be honest."

"And you, Vi?" Lila asked. The twinkle in her gaze declared her faith in what Violet had learned. And perhaps that Lila had already talked to Kate.

"We left to offer assistance, which we did." The innocent statement was met with a snort by Denny who knew Violet well enough to be sure she'd had ulterior motives. Vi ignored his reaction and Jack's doubting expression. She said righteously, "In the process of offering *succor,* we ended up speaking with Marie Bosch, the vicar's daughter."

Kate took over re-capping their morning while Jack's mouth tightened. She wasn't surprised to see him pull his notebook out of his evening jacket, and the notes he took declared that what Violet and Kate had started to uncover would be continued in a more official capacity.

Violet wasn't sure that Jack would be as successful in getting Marie to talk. Without Kate's kind understanding and the girl's apparently inbred desire to obey the peerage—as ridiculous as Violet found that —she was betting that Marie would either lie or cry when the police questioned her.

When they were finished with dinner, Jack had carefully noted the things Violet and Kate had found out before changing the subject back to lighter things. When they'd all finished eating, he led the way to the parlor and made a tray of drinks that were at least three times the number they needed.

He made an array of drinks too. Some were simple, like small glasses of ginger wine, and some were far more complicated, like the rum, chocolate liqueur, and cherry liqueur mixed with cream. Violet wasn't sure that would even be good, but she'd try it even though she was persuaded Jack was mixing haphazardly. Everyone was watching Jack carefully as he put together the drinks and then turned to them with a grin.

"Hide and seek," Jack announced. "Our personal bedrooms are off-limits as well as the servants' quarters and anything outside. While we were eating, the servants were lighting fires and spreading candles throughout the house. Once you're found, come back for a drink and the next round."

Violet met Kate's gaze. Vi hadn't played that game since her school days. Both of them smiled in near unison. She glanced towards Lila and saw she and Denny were both grinning at the idea. Kate slipped off her shoes, and Violet did the same. The t-strap diamond heels were pretty, but they'd make too much noise if one were attempting to sneak around.

"I'll be it." Jack turned and faced the wall. "I'm only counting to one-hundred. Then I'll be finding you." Jack glanced back at Violet, winked, and she grinned.

He'd *try* to find her anyway.

Denny's laugh drowned a quiet aside from Lila and the first few numbers of Jack's counting. "Five…six…seven…"

Violet jumped up, grabbed a cocktail. She glanced back and then hurried towards the door.

"Vi always was the most brilliant of us," Lila said, taking a drink herself. "Why wait to be found for drinks?"

The two of them clinked glasses and darted out of the parlor, separating outside the door. Violet ran up the stairs while Lila stepped into the coat closet. Denny was a breath behind Violet, but he moved towards the library. Vi could hear Kate's laughter as she passed the portrait hall, but Kate didn't come into the room that Violet had selected.

She tried to keep count along with Jack in her head, but she wasn't sure if she'd been steady in her counting when she was running through the house. Violet glanced quickly around the long portrait gallery. The memory of Jack kissing her in the darkness here had drawn her to it. There! The window seat with the curtains. She darted across the room, closing the curtains to hide her location. Perhaps it would seem that one of the servants had already finished that task and the room was empty?

Violet sat down, pulling up her feet so they couldn't be seen under the curtain, then curled onto her side. She propped her head on a palm and sipped her drink with her free hand. She'd taken ginger wine, and it soothed her to breathe it in.

A few minutes later, she heard a shout in the distance then Jack's and Denny's laughter. Footsteps passed the portrait gallery and Kate squeaked loud enough to have Violet biting back a laugh.

Violet was suddenly curious about the drink with chocolate and rum. Would it taste like ice cream with the sweet liqueurs and the cream? Jack had left the ice out of the drinks, so it wouldn't melt while they were playing, but that drink chilled was suddenly a must-try.

The door to the portrait gallery opened. Violet held her breath as she heard heavy footsteps. She had no doubt that Jack was approaching her hiding place. Slowly, silently, she set down her glass and moved to the corner of the window seat. If it was Jack looking for Violet, he'd open at the break in the curtains, and she could dart for the stairs and the parlor.

A moment later, the curtain was flung back nearly in unison with Violet escaping out the side. She darted across the gallery pursued by Jack's laugh. In her stockings, her feet were slipping, so she deliberately let herself slide, speeding through the door with her arms wheeling.

"Careful!" Jack called.

His shout chased her as she pelted out the hallway and down the hall. He gave chase, but Violet careened ahead with a combination of running and sliding. She reached the stairs before him.

With a gasp, she swung one leg over the railing and slid down the stairs on the banister a breath before he caught her arm. She was down the banister long before Jack, even though he was taking the stairs several at the time. She glanced back, saw him halfway down the stairs, winked and darted for the parlor.

Violet slid through the door on the renewed wood floors, slamming the door after herself. She flung herself to the tray of drinks, determined to grab one and be sitting before Jack entered. She snatched a chocolate rum cocktail, dropping onto the chesterfield, fighting her breathlessness as Jack raced into the parlor.

She crossed her ankles as Jack put his hands on his hips and examined her guileless pose. A moment later she glanced around and found both Kate and Denny. They had watched her entrance silently and she saluted them both with a drink.

"I win," Violet said, sipping the drink. It spoke to her, sweet and yummy. Violet already wanted another. She pretended to lean back, but she needed ice. As Jack sat next to her, Violet stood and added ice to her drink before returning to his side. She handed him one of his own creations then lifted her glass to clink it with his.

"What in the world?" Lila demanded as she strolled back into the room. "I declare myself unsurprised that Jack hunted down Violet and left me bemoaning my fate in a closet."

"I found Kate and Denny," Jack said. "Neither of them were as wily as Vi."

"She's a vixen," Denny announced, sipping his drink, adding, "Sneaky even."

"I thought I was venomous," Violet shot back.

"A venomous, vexing vixen of very…ah…other things that start with vee."

"A valiant venture, my versatile chevalier," Lila told Denny, trailing a finger along his back before choosing her own drink. She too selected one of the rum and chocolate drinks.

"Try ice," Violet suggested.

Lila added some, sipped, and paused to close her eyes. She sipped a second time. "That is deliciously divine."

"A decadent drink for my dear darlings." Violet took another sip.

"From *your* dear darling," Jack said. "Dashing dabbler in delicatessens that I am."

Kate lifted her own drink. "Violet, vanquisher of vanishing, victorious and versatile. I surrender."

They laughed and Kate turned on the wireless. The wail of a trumpet filled the room, and Jack pulled Violet into a dance in front of the fireplace. It wasn't quite dancing in the outgoing tides of Cuba's ocean, but Violet found that their hijinks were just what the doctor ordered for her doldrums.

CHAPTER 16

On an average day, Violet did not have too many drinks. The evening before, however, had not been average, and her head was pounding. Violet moaned and plugged her ears as well as she could with one arm wrapped around her head before she rang the bell for Beatrice.

Beatrice opened the door a few minutes later and Violet was lying diagonally across her bed with her eye mask returned to its position.

"Help," Vi moaned.

The maid squeaked. "I'll be right back, my lady."

Violet slipped into a doze until Beatrice returned with coffee, an awful concoction, and aspirin. Violet choked it all down and then curled onto her side until her stomach stopped roiling and her headache faded. She wasn't sure how long it took, but once she could move without wanting to retch, she hobbled to the bath and soaked until she felt human again.

She assumed that no one else would be up before luncheon, but concern for Victor had her tiptoeing across the hall and sticking her head into his room.

Victor was sitting up, dressed, but leaning against his headboard. He had a tray on the bed near him, and he flushed at her appearance.

The tension roiled between them like the storm of the previous night and neither said anything for too long.

Finally, Violet asked, "Feeling better?"

"Indeed. You, however, look like you've battled with death."

"Jack made drinks that had rum, cherry, and chocolate liqueurs with cream. I don't even know how many I had, but they were lovely."

Victor's mouth twitched, then he leaned forward with a serious expression. "I'm a cad."

"Yes." Violet sat down on his bed taking a piece of toast from his breakfast tray.

"An ass."

"Mmm," she agreed.

"A child dressed as a man but more poorly behaved."

"Are you expecting me to disagree with you?" Violet let her frustration over the last few days show on her face, and Victor winced.

"You deserve better. Even when I'm behaving so terribly, I know I need to stop. I…damn it. I'm sorry, Vi. I'm so sorry."

Violet nodded but the tension didn't ease. "I'm glad you're feeling better." Victor watched with a tight mouth as she stood and said, "Take it easy over the next day or two. Just because you're feeling better doesn't mean you're back to yourself."

Victor choked on a frustrated laugh, then sighed as Violet left the room. Perhaps she should have been more understanding and kind. But she didn't feel either of those things. She was angry with him, and she deserved to be angry with him.

She knew he'd likely order her a few books or offer to buy her a new dress in apology, but she could do those things for herself. What she couldn't do was adjust to having a near-perfect brother that occasionally turned into an intolerable nitwit.

Victor followed Violet, calling her name.

Violet paused, looking back and saw Beatrice with Rouge trailing after. Violet clucked to Rouge and went down the stairs with Victor silently following. They reached the gardens and Victor walked by Violet's side. He didn't need to be told she hadn't let things go yet.

He knew.

"I hate myself after I'm sick," he told her, holding out an arm to her.

It was several steps before Violet begrudgingly placed her hand on the corner of his elbow.

"I have something for you. It was going to be for your birthday."

Violet accepted the box. She'd seen it under his arm when she'd finally deigned to look at him. It wasn't, however, whatever was in this velvet box that she wanted.

She stared at him, and he shifted, clearing his throat. "I think you'll love it. I probably never would have made it to our birthday. I've been excited to give it to you."

"Are you saying your guilt has robbed me of a present on a random Tuesday?" Violet couldn't hold onto her anger, but she wasn't quite done with him.

Victor laughed, pausing to look down at her. "Indeed it has. But will it be enough?"

No. To him she said, "I need you to make me a promise."

Victor glanced away and Violet tugged his hand until he looked back to her.

"I am not unaware that I am awful when I don't feel well. I've made the promise to be better before. I...I'm sorry, Violet. You shouldn't have to ask for it again."

In the quiet of her mind, Violet knew that Victor wasn't the only one who was sometimes intolerable. And, it wasn't illness that caused Violet to become a little wild-eyed and sharp-tongued. The cause of her behavior happened far more often than the one time a year the twins might end up ill. She was going to forgive him, as she always did, because she knew what it was like to feel you were being as mad as a hatter and unable to stop yourself.

"It's a different promise," Violet told Victor, convicted by her own thoughts.

"Anything," Victor swore.

She knew he meant it, and the last of her anger about his behavior fled. It made her heart-break over this house worse. Even still, she said, "Promise me that you will never do to Kate what you do to me.

When she's your priority and I'm not around for you to lash out, don't do this to her."

Violet wasn't looking at him anymore. She was scowling at the beautiful rose garden. She hated it despite it being one of the most beautiful gardens she'd had the chance to walk through. In her mind, she could see the future children that Victor had mentioned when he'd succumbed to the drunken sale. She hated the very idea of their existence in *this* garden.

"Are you all right?"

Violet sighed and then admitted. "I seem to have caught the doldrums again."

"Do we need to return to Cuba?"

"I think we should save our return until you're out of rum."

"A day that has come far closer given the way you're green about the gills."

Violet laughed. She had had far too much rum the night before. Victor took a seat on one of the stone benches, and Violet tucked herself next to him. She wrapped her arm around her twin's and leaned her head on his shoulder.

"You hate this house." His voice was low.

She'd never be successful at lying to him now that he was feeling better. "I like the painting of the sour old woman next to Aunt Agatha."

"Shall we put her in our next book?"

"A disapproving spectre?"

"Oooh," Victor joked, "*The Intrepid Virgin and the Disapproving Spectre.*"

Violet shook her head. "It sounds a bit too much like when we visit Father and Lady Eleanor. That could be the title of our reflections upon returning home."

Victor shook his head. "No, no. The return home story is, *The Wild Twins and the Long-suffering Stepmother: A Tragedy.*"

"Stepmother Countess," Violet corrected.

Victor's snort made her smile, and she opened the jewelry case. Her eyes widened as she stared down at the necklace.

"It's not nearly as valuable as the last one—" Victor started.

Violet cut him off. "You know I don't care about that."

Slowly she lifted the long strand from the box. It didn't match what she was wearing in the least, but she could change. She would change. Of course she would. She loved this necklace. It was a perfect, matched strand of turquoise beads as long as her pearl necklaces. It would be an unusual piece, an attention grabber, and it would look amazing with a black dress. Violet placed her finger on an earbob. These matched, but they were combined with diamonds and black jet. Next to them were several bangles, again a combination of diamonds, turquoise, and jet.

"You love it," Victor crowed as she put the bangles on her wrists. There were a half-dozen of them. They all went together, but each was unique. "I thought you would!"

Violet didn't argue as she slowly wound the long strand around her neck, leaving a long loop that reached to her waist and a much tighter one around her neck.

"I love it." She ran her fingers along the perfect beads. Her life would be a challenge of having to decide which of her long necklaces to wear now that Victor had gifted her with her third one.

"I'll never do to Kate what I shouldn't do to you," Victor told Vi. "I promise."

"I love that more," she said truthfully.

Victor stood, pulling Violet to her feet. They started walking again, exploring the rose garden together. Violet paused as she noticed a gardener's toolbox to the side of one of the hedges.

She crossed to it, glancing down. "I wouldn't have thought that Jones would leave his tools out."

"No doubt he expected to return before anything could happen to them."

Violet flinched at the idea, at the concrete proof that the gardener had been caught unawares and had his life stolen. She lifted the tool chest and stumbled. It was heavier than she expected, and when she dropped it, it landed at an angle with the lid opening, spilling out its contents.

Both twins paused as they stared. Under a pair of wicked looking shears, a pile of letters spread across the grass.

"Oh-ho," Victor said as they knelt to gather up a rather shocking number of letters.

"Jack probably needs these," Violet said. She met her twin's gaze and knew they were both thinking the same thing.

"Jack is protective these days. Of you more than anything." Victor's voice was careful.

Violet stared down at the letters and then glanced up her brother. "We *should* tell him…"

"We should," Victor agreed. The smirk on his lips made Violet want to smack his shoulder.

"Later," they said in unison. Victor rose and pulled Violet to her feet. She put the letters into the jewelry box, hiding their existence.

Victor's laugh made Violet pause, as did the flash of guilt she felt, but she knew she wouldn't be giving these letters to Jack until after she had a chance to read them. Wicked? Perhaps. But she'd read quickly and repent her behavior later.

CHAPTER 17

"We're saved, darling," Victor told Violet. "Jack has already left, putting on his official hat and escaping into the fog."

Violet laughed up at her brother, winding her arm through his. "Absolutely fabulous! Now we were never conspiring against Jack. It's not our fault he left before we could tell him."

"We do have a telephone," Victor told her, smirking at her quelling look.

Violet smacked his arm and increased her pace. He strolled behind her as she burst into the breakfast room. Her friends were loading up plates while she glanced around, ensuring that Jack truly was gone. Like Violet, the rest of them looked the worse for wear after the excess of drinks and the late night.

"Violet," Denny moaned, turning slowly and glaring at her with bloodshot eyes. "Your *love* sabotaged us."

Vi paused in loading her plate with sausages and eggs. The sickness in her stomach was gone, and she was ravenous. "Whatever do you mean?"

"I mean that Jack made so many drinks we are all ill. Yet where is the fellow, I ask you? Working, sleuthing, investigating, larking about. He's Holmes, too savvy for us fools. A wily, conspiring fellow."

Violet looked at Lila for clarification. Lila was leaning back. Her face was pale, but beyond that, she was as beautiful as ever. If anything, the paleness of her skin set off her pink lips and red cheeks.

Lila slowly sipped her Turkish coffee. "Denny believes that Jack helped us all dive into our cups to keep you out of trouble today."

Kate paused in loading her own plate and muttered, "The fiend."

Violet, however, laughed. "Too late, my friends. Shenanigans abound. Rally round for mischief, my darlings."

No one perked up.

"Food," Denny said. "I can't shenanigan until I eat."

Violet scrunched up her face, but her whining look didn't make any of her friends give in. They descended on the food as though they hadn't eaten in days. Perhaps the eggs and sausages were assisting in recovery now that they'd probably all had hangover-tonics and aspirin.

Violet's kedgeree seemed to almost melt in her mouth, and the toast sopped up the acid in her stomach. With her third cup of coffee, her mind was clear even if the light was still bothering her eyes. Violet looked up and found that everyone else had shoved their plates away and were sipping cups of coffee or tea.

Lila sat with her eyes closed. "I do feel better. I very much prefer that rum concoction Jack made going down the gullet rather than coming back up."

"I know what you mean," Kate said. "Words of wisdom, my dear friend."

"I only experienced it going down." Violet stirred her coffee as she glanced at her friends. "I believe you should consider upon a touch of temperance."

"Oh!" Lila growled. "You are a fiend, like Jack. This is why he likes you. The evil."

"She's unnatural," Denny added. "Unnatural and venomous. Vexing in the extreme. We've discussed this."

"Not that again," Kate begged. "I am incapable of ingenious insults. Incapacitated, I say."

Denny and Lila groaned at Kate, who smirked and handed her cup to Victor for a refill. "When I return home, I shall dreadfully miss Turkish coffee."

Victor glanced up in alarm, but Kate was examining Violet's necklace. "Oh, I love it. I thought it would be perfect for you when Victor told me he was having it made."

Violet ran her fingers along the necklace and then handed the jewelry box to Lila. "Open it."

"Darling," Lila said, "Victor couldn't keep the secret from anyone but you. We've all seen them."

"Open it," Victor repeated, and Lila lifted a brow, flipped the latch on the box, and uncovered the stack of compressed letters.

"What's all this?" Denny asked, lifting a letter and unfolding it. His head tilted as he examined the pale pink, perfumed paper. "'My darling Philip'..." Denny's mouth dropped open as he flipped to the end of the letter and read, "'With endless faith, love, adoration, and gratitude—Marie.' Is that the child?"

Violet nodded and Victor demanded, "What now?"

Kate filled in Victor on what they'd learned while he was ill while Violet rose to ring the bell. She requested Mr. Morganson, the new butler, to bring paper and a pen and her journal, then started on her fourth cup of coffee. There would be no naps today with that much coffee, but sacrifices had to be made.

They had the servants clear the table before separating the letters into piles. There were four from Marie, two from Mrs. Melody Baker, and seven much shorter notes from Chloe Sandford.

One letter, however, had them all staring. It was from the law office of George, Grendel, and Haliburton and was the start of a divorce.

"Oh my." Violet folded the letter. "Mrs. Jones was using the new marriage act to divorce Jones."

"How scandalous." Kate sniffed. It wasn't judgement so much as shock. She paused for a long moment. "You know, her life has been an endless scandal. She married that man when she probably should and could have done better. Not because of his employment but because of who he was. Then losing her children. His endless affairs. What's one more scandal? This town was going to talk about her regardless."

"The marriage act?" Denny frowned, but he took Lila's hand as he asked, "Is that the one that lets women divorce their husbands for adultery?"

"It is." She squeezed Denny's hand. "Good for her."

"Would you divorce me?" Denny demanded.

Lila rolled her eyes at him. "Have you been stepping out on me, my lad?"

"If I did?"

"You wouldn't have to worry about it, darling." She squeezed his hand. "I would just kill you and inherit your money."

She was joking, but her words paused all of them.

"You don't think…" Victor started.

Kate shook her head a moment later. "She was divorcing him. Why would she kill him?"

"I don't think she *could* have killed him," Violet added. "You saw her."

Everyone else looked at Violet and Kate, who nodded. "She was beaten. Jack had said so, but seeing it for ourselves—it was bad. She was hobbling just to go into her parlor. I suppose given what happened to me and Violet at Christmas, we had a little more understanding than we'd like."

"Regardless," Lila added as she took the letter from Violet to look at it herself, "she was divorcing him. Why would she kill him if she was ending things another way? This tells me that she didn't kill him even if she hadn't been beaten. Everyone in this village knows that he was an adulterer. She wouldn't have had trouble making the divorce go through. If she knew he was violent, she filed for a divorce knowing he would beat her. Yet, she did it anyway."

Violet nodded, playing with her ring. She rose and paced.

Kate took the divorce letter. "What a sad end to a love story."

"I don't disagree, but she didn't kill him. She isn't going to be leaving her house for days, maybe even weeks, while she recovers from whomever beat her. So who did?" Violet flipped through the letters. "Well, let's read them. Denny, you be Marie."

He grinned wickedly. Then, with a high-pitched voice, he read letter after letter. They all choked when Marie referenced an assignation between Jones and the girl.

"How old is she now?" Victor demanded. "You made it sound as though she isn't much older than our Ginny."

"She's not," Violet told him. Their ward was barely into her teen years and far too clever to fall for the nonsense that Marie succumbed to.

She glanced at Kate, who guessed, "Perhaps sixteen or seventeen?"

Victor's expression shifted and Denny stopped reading so mockingly. They were all sick as they heard Denny pour out the girl's thoughts. She had been well and truly in love. In love, manipulated, and now mourning for someone who Violet wished she had murdered herself.

"I think I am finished mourning the Philip Jones that could have been." Violet paced the room with a quicker step. "The problem with this man is that so many people had reason to murder him. The real shocker isn't that he was murdered but that it took so long for him to be removed from this world."

"Indeed," Victor said. "I'm happy enough to help Hargreaves cousin, but to be honest, now I wish I had clued in how the gardener was a snake in the grass."

Kate glanced at Victor, but no one contradicted him. His decision was reasonable but looking back provided so much more clarity.

Violet picked up the letters that Marie had written. Everything about them—the paper, the tone of her thoughts, the revelations enclosed in the words—all alluded to her extreme youth. Melody Baker, however, could not say the same. The woman was married and Violet had seen her kissing the gardener in the orchard. If she hadn't just had an assignation with the gardener when Violet and Jack had seen her—Mrs. Baker had certainly had an assignation with him at another time. They were simply too familiar with each other for Violet to believe anything else. Violet asked Lila to read those letters.

In the end, Violet was unsurprised by what the woman had written. It was clear that there was *something* between them. Mrs. Baker, however, was clever enough to not write anything that would be proof of her infidelity.

Chloe Sandford's letters were flirty at first. They moved from flirty to irritated and then to out and out furious. The last note read only a few short lines. "Stay away from me. Stay away from my family. This type of action will bring you to a sour end."

Violet's brows lifted as her friends broke into chatter. Could Chloe be the woman who was trying to get Jones to talk to her on the street outside the pub? If she was, why had she told him to leave her alone? What had Jones done to make her order him away? Perhaps it was only another round of Marie and Jones, only Chloe wasn't so young and naive.

Violet shook her head. "If this Chloe Sandford is married, this threat could be the reason behind why Jones was killed. After all, Meredith Jones was ending her misery with a divorce. She wasn't able to kill him, regardless, given her state."

"Oh," Kate said. "I sent the doctor to her this morning. I had Mr. Morganson call."

"You're a good woman," Violet told Kate. Vi had forgotten to make that call and hated that she had. "I should have taken care of it myself."

Violet continued to pace the breakfast room as her friends debated which of the women would have been most likely to kill Philip Jones. It was, however, just as likely that someone who cared for one of these women had been the killer. Perhaps even more likely. He had, after all, been stabbed in the wood.

Was that because he had been lured there or followed there? If he had been lured to the wood, it seemed more likely that a woman was the killer. If he had been followed, it seemed more like that someone who loved one of Jones's victims was the killer.

The key, she thought, was who had an alibi. In this case—motives abounded for why Jones was killed. It wasn't really who had a reason to kill him, but who had the chance and the personality to kill him.

"Would you kill someone who manipulated me like Jones manipulated Marie?" Violet asked her brother.

Victor knew that Violet was serious and he leaned back, crossing his fingers over his stomach as he considered. "I—"

Denny snorted and Victor shot him a look to quell him. The expression was unsuccessful.

Violet turned and seated herself across from Victor. She was curious. He was one of the most protective people in her life.

"To be honest, it is hard to imagine that you would fall for this. But...if you were younger. Sixteen-year-old Violet? In love and throwing your life away on a married man? No."

Violet's head tilted while Denny chuckled. Lila smacked his chest to silencing him.

"Murder isn't the tool I would need to use, Vi. Father is an earl, and we are wealthy. There would be so many ways to get rid of someone like Jones. But if I didn't have those options? Maybe."

"To me—Marie is a reason that you kill." Violet played with her ring while her friends turned towards her. "He was ruining her life. Maybe ruined it. How long will it take, do you think, for her to recover from what he has done to her?"

"Quite a while," Lila said. "When I was young and in stupid love with Denny at that point—if he'd turned out to be a bounder? I'm not sure I'd have ever trusted anyone like that again."

"Luckily," Denny told her, leering dramatically, "I was the catch you thought."

Violet ignored Denny as she continued, "If Marie realizes Jones was manipulating her, will she ever trust another man? Will her family ever trust her again? I am almost certain that Jack will approach the vicar today. Today, a good man is going to realize his daughter—"

Denny winced and shifted, glancing at Lila before he turned back to Violet. The vicar was going to realize his daughter had been hurt under his watch. He was going to go to bed that night ruined. The best that anyone could hope for after all of this was that the vicar wasn't the murderer. If he wasn't…could there be someone else who loved Marie and who might have killed Jones? Perhaps some young local boy? Perhaps a brother or an uncle? Someone with less perspective?

Violet shook her head to clear it, then winked at Victor. "I wouldn't murder Jones for you either, brother."

Denny giggled like a child while Lila snorted. Kate reached out and took Victor's hand as he pretended to be wounded. "Victor, darling," Kate said, "I might have murdered him for you. My little delicate flower with the wounded heart and gullible when it comes to those who declare their love."

Victor scowled at Kate's teasing, but there was humor in his gaze. Violet watched her brother realize that Kate wasn't just teasing him— she was inferring she loved him. His gaze brightened and his grin widened.

CHAPTER 18

*V*iolet flipped back in her journal and read over her notes from earlier. She'd made them when she hadn't cared for Jones but had no idea how much she would dislike him after she learned more. The questions were, however, the same. She wrote a new set of notes, starting fresh with what she knew.

Her friends watched her silently as she gathered her thoughts. There was a low murmur of conversation, and both Kate and Lila were writing themselves. Victor had gathered up the book he'd started, flipping through the type-written pages while Denny leaned back and napped in his chair.

Violet started her notes, once again, with Philip Jones.

PHILIP JONES— murdered in the wood. He had some wizardry that allowed him to manipulate women. These women included his wife, who left her higher-class life to marry him, the vicar's teenage daughter, and two married women. Were there more, currently or in the past?

Vi had wondered previously if Jones had found something of value in the house when he'd been the only one around it, but that couldn't possibly be the case. Very unlikely, Violet thought, with all the other motives for him to have been murdered.

The next person on her list was Mrs. Jones. When Violet had made her previous notes, she'd thought that it might be possible that the wife had killed the husband. Violet no longer thought that in the least. Of all the people Violet had met in association with Jones, the only person that Violet felt must be innocent was Mrs. Jones.

It wasn't even because of the loss of her children that made Vi want Mrs. Jones to be innocent, though that would have been enough reason.

Violet stared at her notes with a twisted mouth. Mrs. Jones had been beaten. She had also started divorce proceedings. Did her husband beat her because she was trying to leave him? Did what happen to her somehow cause his murder? Why was she protecting him if he had been the one who hurt her? Respect for the dead? Why wouldn't she say who hurt her?

She considered whether her desire for Mrs. Jones to be innocent was coloring her opinion. Slowly, Violet shook her head and left a note and nothing else next to her name.

MRS. JONES— 'I don't think she killed her husband. But perhaps she knows who did?'

She looked up from her journal, glancing around the breakfast room. Denny snuffled and adjusted, but he was actually sleeping. He clearly had not overdone the Turkish coffee as Violet had. She watched Lila shoot her husband a look at his snuffling, shake her head, and return to her letter. Kate had moved on to her Greek book, but her eyes were closed with the book in her lap. Victor was making copious notes on the manuscript.

Violet returned to her notes.

JOSEPH FRECKLETON— The brother. Violet could easily recall his face as he'd looked down on the graves of the children. At the time, Violet hadn't known his parents were also dead. Were they buried there next to the children?

Did he know his sister had decided to escape her marriage to Philip Jones? Mr. Freckleton had seemed to despise his sister's marriage choice. If her brother were married to someone that Violet despised—even if it were Gerald rather than Victor—she would be relieved to see the unwanted in-law go, though maybe not through murder.

Violet still didn't see why Joseph Freckleton would be the one who killed his brother-in-law unless it was a reaction to his sister's beating. She frowned. She'd seen him in the graveyard close to when Jones had died. If Freckleton had killed his brother-in-law, he'd left him dying and appeared in time to chat with Violet. If it had been him, he didn't show any signs at all of being upset about what he'd done. Violet certainly wouldn't have been able to pull off the casual conversation.

She frowned again at the next name. Violet didn't know anything about James Baker. They had the letters from his wife which, combined with the kiss that Violet had witnessed, made it seem certain that Mrs. Baker had been sleeping with Jones. There was no indication, however, that James Baker knew. If he had, would he have been driven to kill over it?

Violet picked up the letters and glanced them over, looking for dates. Ah...they went back ten months. Perhaps, Mr. Baker had finally realized what was happening with his wife? Unlike the vicar, Mr. Baker wasn't a man of God who had already given over his life to good works. It was easier to believe that any man other than the vicar had been the killer.

Violet had to question whether her prejudices were coming into play again. Perhaps she only wanted to believe that a man who had decided to go into the church truly was what he presented himself to be.

She moved on to the next name.

MELODY BAKER— She was a clever woman, Vi thought, based on her letters. Conniving even. Her letters were vague enough that she could bluff her way out of them.

Violet decided suddenly that after luncheon, she would be visiting the woman and seeing what she could find out.

This time Violet had to add more names to the list, as much as she didn't want to.

FATHER BOSCH— The vicar. He helped Violet happily facilitate the assistance for Mrs. Jones and seemed genuinely glad to hear of the financial help for her. He was also the parent of Marie Bosch. Did he know about Marie and Jones? If the vicar did, was it something that he would kill over?

Violet was sure that Jack was out finding the answers to that question. If the vicar didn't know, he was going to learn today. Sympathy welled in Violet as she thought about it. What a terrible thing for a father to learn!

She wrote the next name with far more opinion than the last few names.

MARIE BOSCH— This was the girl who had given herself to a married man and in doing so had set aside the conventions of her day and the marriage vows she knew he'd taken, and she ignored the story behind the death of the Jones's children. Could a girl manipulated by a man she thought she loved kill that man for what he had done to her?

Violet was sure it was possible. The thing that made her believe Marie was innocent was the way the girl was still such a clear believer in Philip Jones. Marie mourned the man she'd created out of lies and fantasy. If she was still sucked into the lies, why would she have killed him?

Violet had one more name to add.

CHLOE SANDFORD— Her letters were angry. If she was the woman that Violet had seen outside of the pub, she'd been as angry as her letters. Philip had died soon after Violet had seen them.

Chloe was high on Violet's list of suspects. She had been angry and had written threatening letters. Violet very much wanted to find and speak with Miss Sandford.

"Victor," Violet said, closing her journal. "Hijinks? Kate? My doves?"

Kate sneezed and said, "I believe the plague has struck me down."

"Oh?" Victor's head cocked, and he examined Kate carefully. Neither of the twins had realized that Kate had long since closed her book and was simply staring off into the distance. The rest of them had lost their pale skin and the green about their gills look, but Kate's sickly color had intensified.

Violet asked Kate, "Do you need anything?"

"I think I only want to sleep."

Violet shot Victor a look, lifting a brow. He caught the look and ignored Violet as he said, "Gin will come keep your feet warm. I have to admit, he was a comfort when I was sleeping even when I was drugged by my proactive sister."

Kate smiled wanly and agreed to her furry companion while Violet promised to send Beatrice in to check on her while the twins were gone. Victor walked Kate to her room, steadying her when she swayed.

"Lila?" Violet asked.

Denny certainly wouldn't go, so Violet didn't even ask. He hadn't even stopped snoring since they'd started chatting. The big question was whether he was playacting at sleeping so he didn't need to make excuses or whether he really had fallen asleep.

"I'd go. I'd help. I'd be useful and clever." Lila grinned as she added, "But I don't want to."

Violet laughed and Lila returned to her letters. Violet went and changed. She had been wearing a casual dress with slide-on shoes, but she changed into a navy and cream sailor's dress, thick wool stockings, her sturdy shoes, and light jewelry.

Violet put on her cloche hat, pinning it in place, then she added a coat and scarf. It might have been spring, but the weather had been excitable. They'd recovered their electric lighting after the last storm. Every time Violet turned a lamp on, she had a little wish in her heart that it would still work.

Violet headed down the stairs and found that the butler had brought an auto around. It looked a bit dinged up, as though whoever had been driving it had needed spectacles. The auto had already been started, and Victor was standing at the door as Violet descended the stairs.

"Did Beatrice appear for Kate?"

Victor nodded. "Kate got a letter from her mother, and she looked upset. Was it because she was sick? Did I do something else? Mrs. Lancaster half hates me, I think."

Violet shook her head since she didn't have an answer. With Mrs. Lancaster, it could be either. They'd taken Kate with them quite a long time ago and had yet to return her home. Vi was guessing that Victor would prefer that Kate never go home. She wasn't sure she disagreed, but she was guessing Mrs. Lancaster also had a clear preference.

CHAPTER 19

The daily servant had known where Melody Baker lived. Victor had thought ahead well enough to get directions while Violet had thought ahead to have the housekeeper make a generous gift basket for Mrs. Jones.

Violet was the one who wrote the check to help Mrs. Jones get started without her husband. Hopefully, she'd be able to find work to support herself even though her house was paid for. Did she have an additional income from her family? Hopefully, her husband hadn't left her too much in debt. Though the twins had inherited rather extensively after the loss of their aunt, they had struggled to support their lifestyle beforehand.

Melody Baker's home was a small brick house with a smaller garden, but it was all very nice. Victor opened the auto door for Violet and handed her out of the vehicle. The two of them approached the house, glancing at each other. Victor looked worried. Violet guessed she looked like the cat who swallowed the canary.

"How are we going to…ah…"

Violet grinned at him. "Well I was thinking that we'd go ahead and be rude to her. Barge in, demand answers, turn up our noses."

Victor paused in his steps. "Whatever did she do to you?"

Violet fought back a scowl and tried to pretend that she was unaffected, but Victor didn't buy it. "When I met her—after, mind you, seeing her with the gardener—I explained I had been sick. She told me it was the result of heavy drinking. She suggested temperance and a *strict regimen of fruit, vegetables, and exercise.*"

Victor's choked back laugh that had Violet elbowing him in the side.

"This is your fault." Violet truly did blame him and he blushed. "Buying the house the way you did—it will be part of your story here forever."

Victor knocked on the door. "I've been thinking on that. Not sure I like it so much."

"I suppose you are in one of those repent-at-leisure situations."

Victor's expression wasn't all that pleased with Violet's insinuations, but just as they heard the door start to open, Violet hissed, "Channel Stepmother."

Victor shot Violet a glance, but the door opened before he could ask any more questions. They both transformed into snobbish members of the peerage who were deigning to slum with their appearance at this house. Violet would have immediately hated them if she'd found them on her doorstep.

"Ah." Melody Baker's face was disgusted when she took in the twins. Violet glanced the woman over, noting the drop-waist dress. She was fashionable and extremely beautiful. So beautiful, in fact, that Victor looked pole-axed. Violet smirked at Melody.

"Hullo," Violet said. "This is my brother, the Honorable Victor Carlyle."

Victor shot her a quelling look, but Violet would be damned if she wasn't going to enjoy this situation. To Melody Baker, Victor slightly sneered.

Melody Baker lifted a brow. "Was I expecting you?"

"I doubt anyone would expect us," Violet said merrily. "Yet, here we are."

The two women stared at each other until Mrs. Baker finally stepped back and invited them into her front room. She gestured to the seats near the fire, and the twins took them. The furniture was nice, and the house was nice. Violet hadn't truly been sure what to expect. All of her suppositions were based off of one incredibly awkward conversation and seeing Mrs. Baker at the end of an assignation with the gardener.

"Were you just being neighborly?"

"Hardly," Violet said bluntly. Her smile was smooth, but her tone was nearly as venomous as Denny had described her. "We found your letters."

"Mmmm." The judgment in that sound from Victor was enough to have Melody coloring, but beyond that her expression didn't alter in the slightest. "I'm sure I don't know what you mean."

"Did you want me to read your letters to you to assist in your recollection?"

Mrs. Baker paused long enough that Violet was sure she was exploring her options. Her gaze darted to Victor and back to Violet and then she suggested, "Perhaps you could let me see the letter?"

"I have your words here," Violet pulled out her journal and read, "Dear Jonesy..."

"I could read them," Victor said. "Give you a *gentlemen's* perspective on how your husband might feel." The glance he gave Violet told her just how much he enjoyed behaving as their stepmother did. Violet guessed he'd be extra-generous to other people in the coming days.

Mrs. Baker cleared her throat. "If you cannot provide the original letter, I am sure I don't know to what you are referring."

"The original letter, along with letters from *other* women, were given to *Detective* Jack Wakefield and the local constabulary."

Mrs. Baker paled at that statement.

Victor cleared his throat and lifted his brows before he said, "Oh-ho. That's alarming, I would guess."

"Of course, Detective Wakefield—along with myself—saw an interaction between yourself and the gardener. I'm sure that will provide context for your otherwise vague letters." Violet deliberately placed a small amount of emphasis on the word gardener. She might have determined to improve on ridding her prejudices against other

classes, but that did not mean that Violet was unaware those prejudices were common.

"I'm sure I don't know what you mean."

"Come now, my dear," Victor said. "This innocent act only works
for school girls."

"I'm sure Detective Wakefield knows exactly what I mean. Do you
desire to have him investigating your relationship? He will if he
needs to."

Melody Baker's face hardened. "What is it that you're expecting?"

"An alibi." Violet shot back.

"Why would I share that with you? Why do you care?"

"Jack can't leave here until this case is done. Yet, I'm done with this
village."

Victor's gaze darted to Violet, but he didn't say a word. The sneer
on his face faded to blankness, but Violet noted the sour twist to his
mouth. It was, of course, for how they were bullying this poor woman
into giving them details about her life that they had no right to obtain.

"So, you're investigating in order to go home?" Melody's mocking
laughter drove Violet past disgusted straight on to furious. "And you
think I should indulge you, why?"

"I can be discreet, or I can be a rattletrap."

Violet met Melody Baker's gaze. They stared hard at each other,
but Violet didn't give in.

"I don't owe you an explanation."

"I'm not pretending that you do." Violet's voice was smooth and
snobbish. Her stepmother would have been proud. "I'm offering you
discretion in exchange for answers."

Melody was furious, but when Violet waited the woman out,
Melody finally snapped. "What do you want to know?"

"Why Jones?" Victor asked. "Of all men. You are a beautiful
woman."

"He was talented," Melody Baker replied. "A bit of fun in the afternoon while my husband was working. He expected nothing and
wanted nothing other than fun."

"He wasn't going to fall in love with you, then?" Victor asked, having to hide his reaction to what she'd said. Violet would have taken a wager that he was shocked despite his blank expression. He did tend to place women on a pedestal.

"What about his wife?"

"Meredith?" Melody Baker snorted. "If looks could kill, Philip Jones would have been slaughtered by his wife a thousand times over. She hated him before their children died. After? Her hatred was a fire that burned in her so strong you could warm your hands with the heat of it."

Violet shifted. "Mrs. Jones is probably one of the few people who couldn't have killed Jones."

"She'd have killed him long ago, if she was going to do it. Meredith Jones is a weak-willed cipher and nothing more. Jonesy would have left her if she'd owned that house they lived in."

"She doesn't?" Victor asked, glancing at Violet and then directing his expression back to Melody Baker.

"Freckleton owns the house. It was left to his sister, but in a trust that Freckleton handles. All so Jonesy couldn't sell it or mortgage it. The aunt who left the house to Meredith was a wily old thing. They all felt sorry for Meredith after the children died. The choice they tried so hard to talk her out of brought her the misery they expected. No one, however, expected what happened to the children."

Both of the women paused in admiration of the aunt and regret for those poor babies. For a moment, Violet's irritation with Melody lessened.

"I shouldn't be your suspect. I was just…"

Violet tilted her head, waiting for the way the woman would describe her association with Mr. Jones.

"…making friends."

Violet didn't hide her mocking laugh, but Melody wasn't bothered by Violet's reaction. Victor's snort, however, had Melody blushing. It made Vi feel like they were a pair of snakes spitting their venom. An image that Denny would approve of.

"Why are you so focused on me? I suppose that it would be

uncomfortable if my pastime became common knowledge, but not something to kill someone over."

Violet considered the way Mr. Baker had seemed to be upset with Melody when she'd seen them together. It was only recently that women were able to divorce their spouses for infidelity. Mr. Baker, however, had long since had an escape from his wife if he wanted to employ it. It would cause a scandal and probably make life uncomfortable for the couple in this old-fashioned town, but it was still an option.

"What do you mean?" Victor asked, cutting in between the two of them. Violet didn't blame her brother. The instant dislike between Violet and Melody was slowing the conversation down and neither twin wanted to channel their stepmother for long.

"I wouldn't kill Jones. Why would I? He was fun."

Violet suppressed another snort. "Then who do you think did?"

"Thomas Brown. He loved Meredith Freckleton. He's never married. He lingers around her, visits her when Jones isn't around. Brown even puts flowers on her children's graves."

"How often did Brown do that?" Violet asked.

"Why would I know that?"

"What about Chloe Sandford?" Victor asked, his disgust showing.

Melody Baker's mouth twisted.

"We've got letters from her too," Violet warned. "Careful with your *truths.*"

"Careful." Melody Baker laughed. "You are insinuating that you know something you don't. They had a fling. She regretted it. He hated her snobbishness with him, so he played games with her."

Violet's gaze narrowed. "Blackmail games?"

Melody shrugged as though she didn't know. Violet was guessing Melody knew exactly what had been happening.

"Does Chloe Sandford have someone? Is she married?"

"She's a widow. She might have hated Jonesy, but he couldn't really ruin her. People had seen her out with him. It wasn't that Jones was trying to get money out of her or would even have been able to. He was mocking her. He liked to make references about their time together."

"What does she look like?"

"Blonde, too large of bosom, pretty, but on the average side."

Violet was guessing the only accurate part of that statement was blond. She had to have been the woman in the village, considering the reference to Chloe's chest. Violet had seen the curvy woman with Philip. She had also been blonde and lovely. Chloe hadn't been that worried about being seen with Jones. Maybe she only hated him. Maybe her notes were from a woman who had thought she had been in love, realized otherwise, and only wanted to avoid what had happened.

"Does it matter, Vi?" Victor asked with a glance at Melody. "Is there any reason to believe that Thomas Brown got tired of waiting and decided to end his agony? Or Chloe Sandford?"

"Yes," Violet said, "because someone killed him."

Melody shrugged. She didn't seem to be bothered, Violet thought. The woman didn't even seem all that upset that Jones was dead. Was she hiding her feelings, or was something else happening?

Violet glanced at Victor, who very slightly shook his head.

"Where were you when he died?" Victor asked Melody, trying for a more gentle approach.

Melody's grin was smooth when she said, "Mr. Baker and I took the train to visit my mother. We had tickets and my mother will confirm our presence. I'll entrust that, as *honorables,* you'll be honorable to your word."

Violet scowled at Melody. "Your philandering will not be revealed by either of us."

"We never would," Victor said, he rose with an apology on the edge of his mouth but there was a knock at the door.

Violet glanced at Victor, who shrugged. "We'll step out while you deal with your next guest. You can have faith in our capacity to keep your secrets from everyone but the police."

Melody opened the door, and Violet bit her bottom lip when she saw Jack's broad shoulders looming over Melody Baker. Vi's lips twitched at Jack's scowl.

He stepped back. "Mrs. Baker." He looked at Vi. "I need a moment."

Melody smirked at Violet, probably thinking Vi was in trouble. To an extent, she was. But then again—whether he'd said it or not, that tightness about his mouth was because he cared about her safety.

"Vi..."

"Just us girls trading barbs," Violet told Jack, lightly placing her hand on his arm. He shot Victor a look and then pulled Violet to the lane outside of Mrs. Baker's house where they could talk without being heard.

"Violet, whoever killed Jones was a strong and vital individual, or a very sneaky one—or both. I don't want anything to happen to you."

"It won't."

"The image of you hurt and broken after the last time—I don't need to see that ever again."

"Jack..."

"Violet." He cupped her face, blocking her from Melody Baker's view. "I love you."

Her mouth dropped open in utter shock. Of all places...

Her gaze searched his, and she realized it wasn't a willing confession, it was a statement that had been ripped from him.

"I won't lose you. I can't lose you. You must be safe." Each statement was a declaration to the universe. Both a prayer and a vow.

Violet cupped his cheek back, stepping a little nearer to him. "I won't pretend that nothing can ever happen. You and I both know too well that would be a fallacy. I will, however, promise you—if you promise me—that I will be as safe as I know how to be."

He kissed her on the forehead. "I suppose that locking you in the bedroom is out of the question."

Violet smirked, not bothering to answer.

"I want to go home," she told him. "Let's end this." He nodded and she added, "Melody Baker has an alibi, but she was definitely having an affair with Jones. As much as I don't like her, I don't believe she killed him."

"Her husband?"

"She says they both took the train to visit her mother."

"I'll have one of the local boys double check."

Vi lifted a brow at him in a hint, and Jack scowled at her. Begrudgingly he said, "Father Bosch was unaware of his daughter's situation. Both of them, however, have an alibi. They were working with the choir. A good twenty people were aware of their location and could testify to it."

She told him of the box of letters and about Chloe Sandford.

He shook his head before Violet had even finished explaining, "She was one of the choir members. The soprano. The vicar particularly mentioned her as one they were working with specifically. And, of course, you found letters. Funny, isn't it? How you found them after I left?"

Violet laughed, rubbing her thumb over his hand and then leaned into his space, speaking quietly. "Melody Baker inferred that Mrs. Jones may have a lover. A Thomas Brown. Perhaps if Jones beat his wife, Thomas Brown could no longer stand idly by?"

Jack's gaze narrowed. "There are too many people with motives for this case. By Jove! It could have been any of them. The only question is, why now?"

Violet shook her head and admitted, "I could see the lover killing an abusing husband more than anything else. Don't you think?"

"You leave him to me, Violet. Go back to Victor's house. Have tea with your friends, roller-skate in the ballroom. Lila told me she brought the roller-skates while you were ill."

Violet smiled at him. "We'll go check on Mrs. Jones. We have some things for her."

He considered for a long minute, glancing at Victor, before he simply said, "Be safe."

"And you."

CHAPTER 20

"*W*here did this auto come from?" Violet scowled at the vehicle and kicked the tires. Victor stared down at the engine as though he might know how to fix it. Violet knew her brother too well for that. She had no faith in his capacity to fix anything other than a cocktail.

"I am paying for its use," Victor told Vi imperiously. "I am not responsible for its state."

Her laughter had him shooting her a nasty look. She opened the trunk to take the things for Mrs. Jones.

"I am not going to linger while you pretend to fix things. You are a darling brother. I love many things about you. Those things do not include basic mechanical work."

His look was even blacker, but Violet pretended to not see it. "Perhaps go and find someone to deal with this beast?" She winked merrily at him and saluted to head towards Mrs. Jones.

"I'll be after you once I get the auto sorted."

"Delightful! I will see you later, dear brother."

Vi adjusted the large basket in her grip. It had a ham, jellies, tarts, and other pleasantries that might be difficult for her to acquire for herself. It also had an empty journal with a check tucked inside.

More than most would pay, Violet thought, and yet somehow not enough.

Violet had learned how to traverse the village well enough to be able to take a shortcut through a field towards the small lane where a row of economical cottages were lined up under the trees.

About halfway across the field, she heard, "My lady! Lady Violet?"

Violet turned and saw Mr. Freckleton striding towards her. "Hullo, there." Her cheery voice carried over the field, and he grinned at her.

"Hello there. How pleasant to run into you again. I have been quite concerned over you since I heard that you…well…"

"Well…" Violet glanced behind her to avoid the conversation about what she'd seen. She did not want to discuss the dead body and its effect on her.

"Was he yet alive when you found him?"

Violet blinked and then shook her head. Surely, Mr. Freckleton knew better than to ask her such a thing.

"It's better that way," Mr. Freckleton told her. "You wouldn't want to carry his last words with you. Let alone knowledge of who had killed him. That fiend would be a dangerous person to know too much about. May I help you with that?"

Violet shuddered as she handed the basket to Mr. Freckleton. "I fear I wouldn't have been happy to be the last confessor. Anything like that would colour my nightmares. Even if that confession might have ended the investigation into your brother-in-law's death. I am not that…giving."

"It seems to be a difficult case to solve. I fear that the killer will go unknown."

"Never worry, Mr. Freckleton. Mr. Wakefield will solve the crime. He's quite skilled. Sooner or later, he'll find the knave, and all will be well."

"You sound so certain," Mr. Freckleton said. "Pray it be so. I fear that his loss will be the final blow for my sister."

Violet didn't get that feeling at all. If anything, people seemed to be a little relieved on Mrs. Jones's behalf. Though no one wanted to say,

'Thank goodness, he's dead,' Violet was convinced that they were all thinking it.

Violet wasn't going to argue with the lie that Philip Jones was a good man.

"I feel like we've become friends," Mr. Freckleton told Violet. His tone had her pausing for a second. Had they bonded over the graves of the children? Her with empathy and him with revealing his grief? Yes. Friends, however? That was reaching.

She glanced at him, her expression freezing a little before she pointed across the field to a family of bunnies. "I hope to hear that your sister is doing better? When I stopped by on behalf of my brother, she seemed quite upset."

Mr. Freckleton cleared his throat. "Perhaps my statement about our friendship has made you somewhat uncomfortable. I don't wish to be forward, but as your elder, as a man of the world, and a more experienced individual, I wonder if I might offer you a word of advice?"

Violet's rush of fury blinded her for a moment. Older? Yes. A man of the world? In this village? Her heart was rampaging with doubts. A man? Was that a compelling difference between them that allowed him to give her—a stranger—life advice? Because she was female? Violet did not believe that in the least.

For the sake of peace, she smiled brightly, waiting for his unwanted comments. If she were a cat, her hair would have been standing on end.

"Marrying below your class, my dear, causes trouble and shame for your family. I have heard that you are quite close to the London bobbie. Long-term happiness includes accepting…"

Violet sniffed, trying to hide her reaction.

"…even embracing that the way you were raised, and what you expect from your life cannot be delivered by some two-bit copper."

The rage she felt, it made that earlier rush of anger seem like nothing. Hearing Jack insulted after he'd finally told her he loved her, by Jove! She was having a hard time not boxing Mr. Freckleton's ears.

"I can see that I have bothered you." Mr. Freckleton smiled condescendingly. "It's difficult to hear the unfortunate truths. My sister has —had—spent most of her married life unhappy."

"I'm sorry to hear that," Violet started.

Mr. Freckleton held up a hand to silence her, and Violet stopped in shock. "We will, of course, mourn poor Philip, it is better that she has no one—that this tragedy has come to its culmination. She could have been happy. If she'd been wise enough not to throw her life away."

Violet placed her hand on her chest as they entered the lane from the field. She was internally shocked and horrified that Freckleton felt as though the loss of the children was somehow anything other than tragic. "I'm startled."

"I shouldn't have been so blunt in my opinions," Mr. Freckleton stated. "I should have known better. I suppose that with what poor Meredith and I have been facing, with the loss of my brother-in-law, I have been looking back at the tragedy and wishing things could have been different. I thought maybe I could help you."

"Thank you for sharing your experience," Violet told Mr. Freckleton. Her voice made clear the extent of her gratitude.

"Ah…yes…I have offended you. Love makes us so blind."

"I wonder if you've met Mr. Wakefield?"

"Do you think that I have never met a yard man before?"

"I think that you haven't met Jack Wakefield and you've made assumptions about him based upon the fact that he's a brilliant investigator and tends to lend a hand when needed."

"Having a position at Scotland Yard is not lending a hand, my dear. This is one of those lies that men tell the women they're trying to manipulate into marriage. I assure you, he has his gaze on whatever money you might have, your connections, and nothing more."

"Mr. Freckleton!" Violet's half-hearted attempt at patience faded, and her fury was clear in her voice. "I am assured that you have not met Mr. Wakefield or realized that he is—in fact—of my own class. The question is not whether he is good enough for me, but why such a talented, well-connected man respected not only for his family but for his skills would bother with a frivolous good-for-nothing like myself.

I can assure you, my good man, that Jack Wakefield will be the one slumming should we marry."

Mr. Freckleton's slight laugh told Violet that he was humoring her. Violet had no interest in hearing the rest of his nonsense.

They'd reached the cottage and Mr. Freckleton opened the door and invited Violet inside. Before Violet could excuse herself, she saw Mrs. Jones stumble into the room. She froze as she stared at her brother. Violet froze as she stared at Mrs. Jones.

She wasn't wearing her veil, and Violet could see the split bottom lip, the large black eye, the crooked nose. Her face was swollen and looking at it made Violet's own face hurt. Her heart, however, hurt when she saw the stark terror on Mrs. Jones's face.

"Oh my," Violet said, crossing to her and gently wrapping an arm around her waist. "Let's get you back to bed, darling. I can see that I have come just in time."

Mrs. Jones said nothing. Her gaze was fixed on her brother, but she let Violet help her to bed. She was silent except for little gasps as Violet helped her move through the house. It was really only a trio of rooms. The small front room, the small kitchen area, the small bedroom with a little center space that served the purpose of a hallway.

"Mr. Freckleton," Violet said merrily. "This is one of those moments for the girls. Perhaps you would be so kind as to make your sister a sandwich. I shall help her with her nightgown. Darling, do you need a new one?"

Mrs. Jones was trembling and her expression told a tale that her words hadn't. She nodded silently, her gaze jumping from Mr. Freckleton to Violet and back again.

Things were coming together in Violet's head. This man had just lectured Violet based off of his prejudice about Jack, using Mrs. Jones's experience. Freckleton was so old-fashioned he felt free to tell a person he didn't know that she should not marry based off of rumors. Violet hadn't thought that he'd have killed Philip Jones. Except...except...except the divorce.

The divorce! Violet hadn't taken the scandal seriously. Victor had become notorious for making a drunk purchase. Everyone Violet had met had known about it. How would they treat a woman who used the new marriage act to leave her husband?

Why had the beating happened? What if Mr. Freckleton had attempted to dissuade his sister from leaving Philip? What if she took the beating but refused to give in to him. What if…Violet's heart was racing and she was trembling nearly as much as Mrs. Jones.

Violet had actually thought ahead to put a nightgown and kimono in the basket of items for Mrs. Jones. Violet left the bedroom with Mrs. Jones sitting on the side of the bed while she darted into the small kitchen area to take the non-food items from Mr. Freckleton. She shot him a glance and noticed his fierce expression.

Violet helped Mrs. Jones pull off the nightgown she was wearing. Her ribs were wrapped with cloth. Violet took in the bruises on her chest and side, the large bruise on a thigh that was the size of a man's hand—she noted every mark and said nothing. Violet slipped the nightgown over the woman and followed with the kimono to provide some luxurious warmth. Then Violet had Mrs. Jones sit on the bed, putting up her feet while Violet brushed her hair for her.

Before Mrs. Jones lay down, Violet handed her a washcloth to freshen up as well as she could. She'd have tried for chatter, but the painful squeaks from Mrs. Jones and the bruises left Violet struggling to not shriek at Freckleton and find a blunt instrument to teach him his own painful lesson.

"There now," Violet said, kindly. "A bit of tea and you'll feel a little better. I find being fresh is the first step to feeling well."

Mrs. Jones had let out a silent stream of tears through the entire process, and Violet carefully gave the woman a gentle smile along with her handkerchief, helping her to lie down.

"Be careful," Mrs. Jones breathed. Her voice was so low that Violet had to think on what she'd heard before she understood what the woman had said.

Violet smiled brightly and glanced back. The door was still closed, but Violet was guessing Mrs. Jones whispered for a reason. This was a tiny cottage with close quarters. Did it also have very thin walls? Vi gave the woman a careful nod.

Keeping her voice bright and merry, she asked, "Are you hungry, dear? I fear I am a very poor domestic, but I believe I could make you some halfway drinkable tea."

Mrs. Jones shook her head, but Violet nodded, giving the woman a firm look. It wasn't to force her to have unwanted food, it was to stall for time. Victor would come sooner or later, and they'd be far safer. Until then, it would be bright, merry stalling.

"Dear one," Violet told her, knowing Mr. Freckleton was listening. "I believe that you need your rest. Our bodies are amazing, aren't they? I was nearly as bad as you around Christmas after quite a dramatic mishap. Now I'm back to myself. You just need time. Have hope, it gets better."

Violet found the strength to keep up a constant stream of chatter now that she couldn't see the bruises as well. She opened the window, looking for anyone who could help, but all was empty in the garden Violet could see over the fence. Violet adjusted the blankets and folded an afghan. She was desperately trying to decide what to do.

Did she dare leave Mrs. Jones with her murderous brother? Would he kill her if Violet made it clear that she was coming quickly back? Or did she stall until Victor arrived and somehow make him understand what they'd learned?

Mr. Freckleton! Violet had seen him in the graveyard. He could have stabbed Jones and made his way *easily* to the graveyard. Just because she hadn't seen where he'd come from didn't mean he hadn't stepped off the same trail she'd discovered the body on.

What if he'd murdered Jones and then gone to the graveyard to lay flowers on the grave? Was that why he'd approached Violet? Did he want to be seen while Jones was possibly dying? Until he'd lectured her, Violet wouldn't have thought that there was a reason for Freckleton to have killed his brother-in-law.

At least not since the crime was committed so long after the death of the children. She supposed, however, that if he had realized that his sister was going to divorce her husband, that might be what pushed him. That additional scandal might be the last straw. Her feeling that he might be the killer was cementing into a certainty. How could he not be given Mrs. Jones's fear?

Mr. Freckleton was standing in the doorway when Violet glanced up, and she yelped. "Oh, Mr. Freckleton, I didn't see you there."

She laughed, but she didn't sell her humor. He watched far too carefully as she came to take the sandwich. He didn't quite let go of the plate, making her pull a little, then smiled when she paled.

He was playing with her. Like a cat with a mouse. Violet brought the sandwich to Mrs. Jones, who knew that they were in trouble. Violet started chattering as she told Mrs. Jones that she'd brought jellies and biscuits and started offering sweets.

"Oh," Violet said happily. "I did bring some of the early berries. Do excuse me, Mr. Freckleton. Let's entice your sister to a little something, shall we? Did you see the chocolates? Perhaps you could help me find them?"

He followed her, pacing like a jackal. Violet dug through the basket, looking for the bowl of berries and arranged them for Mrs. Jones. While Violet worked, she grabbed a knife to cut a string on one of the boxes of treats they'd put in. They had put together the strangest mix of things. The kimono and nightgown from Violet. Ginger wine and brandy that Victor must have sent down. Food from the kitchens. Chocolate from Denny, who could always be counted on to have several boxes with him. There were several novels from Kate. None of it was enough.

"I'll just add a chocolate, don't you think?" Violet smiled up at Freckleton. "I found them to be quite enticing when I was unwell. Do be a dear," Violet asked him, "and get your sister one of the sofa pillows. I think she'd do well with some support while we persuade her through some of this food."

Mr. Freckleton turned, crossing to the chair. The way the doors were open let Violet see him the whole way into the front room. While he was turned away, Violet slipped the small kitchen knife into the pocket of her skirt. How grateful Vi was to have had her skirt cut with sensible pockets.

144

She smiled up at him as she carried the second plate to his sister, knowing he was watching her as she moved through the house. Did he know what she suspected? If he didn't, perhaps Violet could go for help and leave Mrs. Jones. If he did, neither of them were safe. She couldn't be sure, and the risk…no…Violet couldn't leave Mrs. Jones. Vi needed to stall until Victor appeared, despite the fear that was increasing with each breath.

Violet went back into the bedroom with Mr. Freckleton following. Vi tucked the sofa pillow behind the woman and handed Mrs. Jones the small plate with the berries and two truffles before turning to Mr. Freckleton.

"I declare," Violet said. "I'm not sure it's wise to leave your poor sister alone. I wonder if I can persuade you to bring my brother to me? I feel certain that our new housekeeper is longing for someone to fuss over."

"Oh," Mrs. Jones said with the smallest shred of hope in her voice.

"I assure you I can take care of my sister. My housekeeper will return here soon. Meredith will be more comfortable in her own bed."

"There is a lot to be said," Violet told him cheerily, "for resting in someone else's home where the sight of the dust on the windowsill or the dishes at the table don't make you feel as though you must take care of things. No, I am persuaded she must allow us to care for her."

"Indeed," Mr. Freckleton snapped, all traces of friendliness fleeing, "I am more than capable."

"Of course you are," Violet answered, trying to convey an easy acceptance. "I'll sit with her until your housekeeper comes then. I believe we ladies need each other during times like these."

Mr. Freckleton didn't argue, and Violet added, "There is a chill in the air today. My good sir, I think I must insist that your sister have a fire."

He attempted at a smile, but he failed. His cold eyes made Violet think of a reptile. As he left the bedroom, Violet crossed again to Mrs. Jones. She whispered as low as possible, "Your brother was the one who beat you?"

Mrs. Jones didn't answer, but her gaze was wide and terrified.

145

"I understand," Violet said significantly. "Do not worry, my dear."

Violet paced the room as she considered what to do. She was certain she had found the killer, and she was certain that Mrs. Jones was in danger. Possibly both Mrs. Jones and Violet were in terrible jeopardy.

A few minutes later, Mr. Freckleton came back into the house and with him came the sound of her twin's deep laugh.

"Hullo, love," Victor said. Did he see the rush of relief on her face? The way she had been pacing and had come to a sudden, gladdened stop? Violet hoped so. "The auto is being handled. I have come to walk you home."

Violet tried to smile, but she failed. Victor's gaze widened as he realized that Violet was upset. She glanced at him and then beyond Victor to Mr. Freckleton. They were still in the front room, but Violet was apparent in the doorway of the bedroom.

"I've been trying to persuade Mr. *Freckleton* to let us care for his sister. I think Mrs. Morganson and Beatrice would delight in fussing over his sister, but he tells me no."

"Your brother understands," Mr. Freckleton said sharply, "that it is my place to look after my sister. I doubt he'd allow another to care for you."

Victor had caught the slight emphasis of Violet on Freckleton's name, and her twin immediately understood. His mask fell into place. The spaniel he normally pretended to be cemented into position, but Violet saw the lion underneath.

"Mrs. Jones," Violet said. "Now is the time to say if you wish to come with my brother and me. We'd be happy to fuss over you." Her gaze widened and Violet said, "We can *help* you."

"I assure you," Mr. Freckleton said. "I have the capacity to care for my sister easily. She will be more comfortable with me."

Slowly, tremulously, Mrs. Jones said from her bed, "I think I should like to be fussed over by their servants, Joseph. Your house-keeper doesn't come for the full day. I am *quite* unwell."

Violet would have squeezed Mrs. Jones hands for daring to speak up with such a challenge in front of her, but they were bruised.

"Victor," Violet said with the same weight that demanded he side with her.

He nodded and turned to the other man. "Come now, Freckleton. We can't understand the ways or wants of women. They're irrational creatures you know, but we must bow to their wants."

Violet ignored both men as though the matter were resolved and turned back to the bed. "What would you like to bring?"

"Nothing. It doesn't matter," Mrs. Jones whispered, her voice but a whisper. "I...don't know why you're helping me, but I'm grateful."

Violet heard a crash and the two women's gazes met, both of them terrified. Vi had waited for the sound of her brother saying all was well, but she knew he wouldn't have attacked if he could avoid it. Instead, there was pure, haunting silence.

Neither of the men were in the view of the doorway anymore, and Violet couldn't see her brother. She was certain he wasn't the one who had attacked. He wouldn't have been.

"Oh, God," Mrs. Jones moaned.

Violet slowly straightened. If it had been Victor doing the knocking about, he would have called out to Violet. Therefore...it was time for Violet's lioness to come out. She met Mrs. Jones gaze and pressed a finger to her lips.

"Everything all right?" Violet called brightly as she glanced frantically about for a larger weapon, but there was nothing except the small kitchen knife in her pocket. Violet certainly did not want to get close enough to have to fight him in close quarters.

"Hardly," Mr. Freckleton replied from the front room. As he spoke, he crossed to the bedroom. "Things have come to an unfortunate head. I am sorry, Lady Violet, but your interference has left us in a precarious position."

Violet smiled cheerily and asked, "How do you imagine this will go? The best that you can do is flee before Jack catches you. If you hurry, perhaps you will reach the border."

"I won't flee. Which will require your unfortunate demise."

"Jack knows we're here."

"Lying will do you no good."

"Jack not only know we're here, he *does* love me. If you hurt me, you will never run fast enough or far enough."

"He loves your money. The moment his chance at it is gone, he'll move on to the next spoiled fool."

"We went to see Melody Baker," she said, stalling for time. "She was sleeping with your brother-in-law. She suggested that Thomas Brown might be the killer. I imagine a man who has loved your sister for a long time must know that you were the one who hurt her. Maybe he has a good idea about you being the one who killed Philip. Do you think that he won't suggest you? He will. Jack will come here to confirm. He'll find you, and your chance of escape will be nil."

Mr. Freckleton paused.

"Thomas will send him here," Mrs. Jones told her brother, her voice shaking. She had pushed herself upright and swung her legs to the side of the bed but remained sitting. Violet's mind was focused on her brother, but she couldn't go to him when Freckleton had revealed his colors. "He remembers how you used to hurt me. He wondered the first time he saw what had happened if it was you. Even Thomas knew that Philip wouldn't have hurt me like this."

"He's a fool for wanting you after you soiled yourself. He was always too good for you," Mr. Freckleton shouted. He lunged then, grabbing Violet and swinging her around to hold her against his chest. "This is your fault, Meredith. Your fault that Philip had to die. Your fault about the children. Your fault about these two meddlers who will be your next victims."

"Stop it, Joseph. What are you going to do? Kill us all?" She had pushed herself to her feet, but the movement was clearly painful. Violet could expect no help from Mrs. Jones.

"If I do, lay it at your feet, *sister.*" He used the word 'sister' like a curse.

Violet could hear Jack in her head, telling her how to break free. She felt the pressure of Mr. Freckleton's hands on her body, but he didn't take her seriously. She bet she thought he'd already won. Victor was down, Violet was captured, Mrs. Jones could do very little. He would learn how wrong he was.

'Distract him,' Violet mouthed to Mrs. Jones.

She didn't react, but Violet knew the woman had seen what Violet had said. "Why do you care so much about my life? We both agree. I destroyed my life. By Jove, Joseph! Why ruin yours?"

"There's nothing left but you," he shouted. "Nothing. No children. No niece, no nephews, no parents. Nothing but *you*. The curse of my life. I'll be damned if you throw away the last measure of our reputation."

"So you're going to kill us? What does that leave you with?" Freckleton pulled Violet back, yanking her into the kitchen, and Mrs. Jones followed at her fastest hobble.

Violet couldn't see his face, but she could feel him loosen his grip. She lifted her arms up and out as Jack had taught her, spinning in his arms, and then kneed him right in his gentle bits. He squeaked as Violet scratched her nails down his face, digging her thumb into one eye. She jumped back just as Mrs. Jones slammed her frying pan down on her brother's head. It had been only a step away—the benefit of a tiny house.

"Oh my!" Mrs. Jones cried, holding her ribs. She hobbled back, leaned against the wall, and wept.

Violet glanced towards the front room and her brother, but all she could see was his long, motionless legs. Everything in her demanded that she run to him, but she couldn't risk Mr. Freckleton recovering while she checked on Victor. She took off her scarf and the knife out of her pocket, cutting it into quick strips, then used those strips to bind Mr. Freckleton.

Mr. Freckleton was moaning and down, but Violet only had a minute to get him bound before he would be able to overpower her. She used the same knots that Victor and Violet had researched for one of their books. As soon as she had him tied up, Violet darted through the doorway to Victor. She placed a hand on his shoulder, turning him over to the magical sound of his groan.

"Victor!"

He lifted his hand, pressing it against the back of his head as he blinked rapidly. "I'm...things are a bit blurry, Vi."

"I've got you," she said, pulling him to a sitting position.

"Vi, where is he?"

"I did it! I'm a woman among women. Just like you and Jack taught me. He grabbed me, I broke free, and I got him right in his goods. Then his sister got him with a frying pan. We are both women among women!"

"Good girls," Victor groaned, rubbing his head. "We need Jack."

"I've got the fiend tied up." Violet pressed the knife into Victor's hand. "Stab him if he moves. Don't be kind."

She pulled him to his feet, helped him to a chair over Mr. Freckleton's body, and then handed Mrs. Jones the frying pan again.

Violet told the woman, "Hit him if he moves. Don't be kind. Don't risk my brother."

Mrs. Jones nodded. "Of course. Yes."

"I'll be as fast as possible." Violet ran out of the house, heading down the lane. As she did, her gaze darted, looking about for help. She caught sight of an auto coming her way and waved her hands overhead. She'd take help from whomever she could. When the vehicle stopped, she ran forward, but Jack was already stepping out.

"Jack!"

"Are you all right?"

She shook her head, grabbing his hand and pulling him towards the cottage. "It's Freckleton."

"I know," he said.

"He attacked Victor, he beat his sister, he grabbed me. We struggled and...I...well...I tied him up."

"What the devil!" the local constable said, rushing after them. "Well...you could knock me over with a feather. Always seemed like a good fellow to me."

Neither Jack nor Violet bothered to reply. The door of the cottage was thrust open and the sight of Mr. Freckleton attempting to free himself in the kitchen while Mrs. Jones wept was all Jack needed. He crossed to the killer while Violet told the constable, "I'm rather good at knots. Don't worry."

"If she does say so herself," Victor added for Violet, smirking when she shot him a look. She couldn't help but touch his wound. "I'm fine, Vi darling. All is well."

All being well was a bit of an exaggeration. Violet stepped away from her brother to help Mrs. Jones back to her bed. They left the bedroom door open so they could hear Mr. Freckleton cursing as he was hauled out of the house, and then Jack came to check on the two of them.

"You were supposed to be safe delivering a care package." Jack's announcement was rather unnecessary, Violet thought, but she stood up and tucked herself into his side.

"I was safe. I was safe because you and Victor made sure that I know how to keep myself safe."

His lips dropped onto her head, and she felt the safest she'd ever been there in his arms.

CHAPTER 21

*V*iolet woke several days later to the sound of her bedroom door opening. She sat slowly up, pushing back her eye mask, and watched Victor cross the floor to her bed. His eyes were wild as he said, "Kate's mother called her home. She got the letter before she got ill and she's only just told me."

Violet's mouth twisted as she saw her brother dig his fingers into his hair, wincing at the pain from his bruised skull.

"What are you going to do?"

"What can I do?" he demanded.

Violet's lips twitched at the answer, but she waited for Victor to realize.

"Oh," he said. He didn't look any less distressed as he cleared his throat, rubbing the place over his heart. "What if she's not the one?"

Not the one! Violet had to hide another grin as she stared at her brother.

"Does the idea of her leaving make you hurt?"

He nodded slowly.

"If you have to imagine the rest of your life without her…"

"Bloody hell, Violet. I— "

"Then you need to do something about it before the rest of your life is spent thinking about how vastly you ruined it."

He nodded, almost drunkenly. His eyes were still wild, but there was an edge of conviction to them.

"Then you know what to do."

~

VIOLET DRESSED QUICKLY, in a race against Kate, who Vi wanted to beat to the breakfast room. She left off all makeup and jewelry and threw on the first dress she could find. When she reached the breakfast room, only Victor and Jack had arrived. Jack had made a plate and had a cup of tea. He had clearly been reading the newspaper before Victor had joined him. Victor was pacing frantically from one end of the breakfast table to the other, muttering to himself.

Jack lifted a questioning brow at Violet, but she smirked in reply. She wouldn't be scuttling Victor's play. She made herself a quick plate and seated herself next to Jack. Jack's English breakfast tea was still steaming as he sipped it. His plate was loaded with breakfast, but neither Jack nor Violet were eating as they watched Victor. Her twin might have walked leagues by the time the next person entered the room, but it was only Denny.

He examined Victor for a moment, harrumphed, and silently created himself a loaded breakfast plate.

"I hope Lila gets here before the show begins," Denny said. "Perhaps, my friend, you could delay until my Lila appears."

Victor didn't even reply. Lila, fortunately, arrived next. She took one look at Victor, laughed, and sat down with the tea and toast Denny had already acquired for her.

"Oh, I was worried he'd do it without us," Lila told the others. "Looks like he won't last for some romantic setup with candles and roses. Jack? Violet's an author. She's got a vivid imagination."

Violet started, staring at Lila, who laughed evilly. Violet glanced at Jack, but his attention was directed at Victor. She wasn't even sure he had heard Lila. He certainly didn't react as though he had.

They all heard the footsteps next. Victor pushed his hands through his hair, then frantically straightened his jacket. He glanced at Violet, who winked at him. Slowly—as the door to the breakfast room opened—they all stared at poor Kate, who came in to everyone's fixed attention.

Kate had recovered from her illness, but she was still a bit pale. Violet had felt for some time that Kate was one of the loveliest people she had ever seen. That might, however, be because Violet knew that Kate was absolutely fabulous. Under their concerted attention, Kate slowly blushed, heightening her own beauty.

Kate glanced around, took in the sight of Victor, who was staring at her.

Violet pressed her lips together to keep herself from telling Victor to get on with it. The poor lad was gawking at Kate as though he'd never seen her before.

"Kate," he said, his voice almost pleading.

She tried smiling at him. Her eyes were big and upset.

Violet crossed her ankles as she leaned forward. As she did, Jack placed a hand on her back.

"Good morning," Kate said to Victor before glancing at the others. "Did Victor tell you? Mother would like me to come home."

Maybe she thought that they were all staring because of the news of her departure.

"Kate..."

Denny choked back a laugh, keeping himself silent enough that Kate and Victor didn't notice. Violet glanced at Jack and found his gaze was on her rather than the couple. She smiled to him, turning back to her brother as Jack slowly took his hand from her back to take her hand in his.

"Kate...don't go," Victor begged, crossing to her. He held out a hand to her, and Kate placed her palm on his. "By Jove, stay with me."

Kate hesitated at the broken begging, but he hadn't done it. Get on with it, Violet wanted to say. Kate needs the words.

She slowly started to reply, but before she could tell him that she needed to go home, Victor dropped to his knee.

At the movement, Kate's mouth fell open. Slow understanding crossed her face and her gaze widened. She breathed jerkily as Victor used the hand he'd taken to pull Kate a little closer.

"I can't…I don't…I…" Victor glanced at Violet as though begging for help and then jerked his attention back to Kate.

Denny laughed—not able to hold it back this time—but the couple didn't notice. Both of them had their wide, expressive gazes fixed on each other.

A tear slipped down Violet's cheek. Was there anything more beautiful than such clear love?

"Please…" Victor said, stumbling again. "Please stay with me."

Slowly, Kate licked her lips. Violet found herself sending her intense thoughts to Victor. 'Ask her,' Violet was ordering him mentally. 'Say the words.'

Finally, he did.

"I am lost without you, Kate. I love you. I adore you. I need you. My God, make *me* your home. Be mine. Be my wife, my… everything…*please.*"

Kate's teeth dug into her bottom lip. Tears were slipping down her cheeks as well as Violet's. "Yes!"

"Oh, thank God!" Victor leapt to his feet and pulled her into his arms.

"Hurray!" Violet called, joining in the congratulations from their friends. They went unheard. Victor and Kate had eyes only for each other.

Violet wiped away a tear with shaking fingers as Kate pulled back from Victor.

"Would you do something for me?" Kate asked.

"Anything."

"Put Violet out of her misery and get rid of this horrible house and save us from this horrible village."

"Hurray!" Violet laughed.

Victor nodded almost frantically. "Whatever you want. Of course. Certainly. Should have done it already."

"Breathe, man," Denny advised, but he went unheard once again.

~

"ARE YOU ALL RIGHT?" Jack asked as Violet visited the gardens with him one last time. A part of her already regretted leaving behind the unicorn hedge and the beauty of the roses. It didn't win against the part who was delighted to leave, though.

"Yes," Violet told Jack. "I am well."

"Kate and Victor…"

Violet smiled assurance to Jack. She could see that he was worried that she was somehow jealous of Kate. Not of Kate but of Victor's affection for his love. It seemed to have been the worry of everyone who knew them since they were old enough to imagine them married.

Not for the last time, Violet explained. "Isn't she lovely? I feel as though Victor has given me the best gift ever."

Jack lifted his brows in question.

"Another sister. One I don't have to look after as I do Isolde. I am excited for what comes next."

Jack cupped her cheek, leaning in to kiss Violet's forehead as he said, "As am I."

The END

Hullo, my dahlings, hullo! You are all ab fab! Are there words enough for how much I love you for reading my books and giving me a chance? Writing books for a living is simply the bees knees! Almost as wonderful are reviews, and indie folks, like myself, need them desperately! If you wouldn't mind, I would be so grateful for a review.

The sequel to this book, *Murder in the Shallows* is available now.

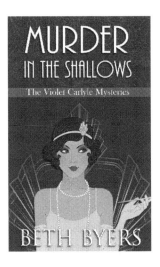

July 1924.

Violet and Jack go for a simple day on the water. They little expect their day of sun and fun to end with finding a body in the water.

The mystery of what happened to the young man in the shallows posses them both, and they unite in their desire to find out more. Will they be able to discover why Jack's one-time friend was killed? Who would have done this and why?

IF YOU ENJOY HISTORICAL MYSTERIES and are interested in my new series, *The Poison Ink Mysteries*, please keep on flipping for a snippet of the first novel, *Death by the Book* which is available now.

July 1936

When Georgette Dorothy Marsh's dividends fall along with the banks, she decides to write a book. Her only hope is to bring her account out of overdraft and possibly buy some hens. The problem is that she has so little imagination she uses her neighbors for inspiration.

She little expects anyone to realize what she's done. So when *Chronicles of Harper's Bend* becomes a bestseller, her neighbors are questing to find out just who this "Joe Johns" is and punish him.

Things escalate beyond what anyone would imagine when one of her prominent characters turns up dead. It seems that the fictional end Georgette had written for the character spurred a real-life murder. Now to find the killer before it is discovered who the author is and she becomes the next victim.

IF YOU WANT to read a couple of short stories about the Cuban vacation. Please see *New Year's Eve Madness* and *Valentine's Madness*. Neither story is necessary to understand the events in the next book.

.   .   .

IF YOU WANT BOOK UPDATES, you could follow me on Facebook.

DEATH BY THE BOOK PREVIEW

CHAPTER ONE

GEORGETTE MARSH

Georgette Dorothy Marsh stared at the statement from her bank with a dawning horror. The dividends had been falling, but this…this wasn't livable. She bit down on the inside of her lip and swallowed frantically. *What was she going to do?* Tears were burning in the back of her eyes, and her heart was racing frantically.

There wasn't enough for—for—anything. Not for cream for her tea or resoling her shoes or firewood for the winter. Georgette glanced out the window, remembered it was spring, and realized that something must be done.

Something, but *what*?

"Miss?" Eunice said from the doorway, "the tea at Mrs. Wilkes is this afternoon. You asked me to remind you."

Georgette nodded, frantically trying to hide her tears from her maid, but the servant had known Georgette since the day of her birth, caring for her from her infancy to the current day.

"What has happened?"

"The…the dividends," Georgette breathed. She didn't have enough air to speak clearly. "The dividends. It's not enough."

Eunice's head cocked as she examined her mistress and then she said, "Something must be done."

"But what?" Georgette asked, biting down on her lip again. *Hard.*

CHARLES AARON

"Uncle?"

Charles Aaron glanced up from the stack of papers on his desk at his nephew some weeks after Georgette Marsh had written her book in a fury of desperation. It was Robert Aaron who had discovered the book, and it was Charles Aaron who would give it life.

Robert had been working at Aaron & Luther Publishing House for a year before Georgette's book appeared in the mail, and he read the slush pile of books that were submitted by new authors before either of the partners stepped in. It was an excellent rewarding work when you found that one book that separated itself from the pile, and Robert got that thrill of excitement every time he found a book that had a touch of *something*. It was the very feeling that had Charles himself pursuing a career in publishing and eventually creating his own firm.

It didn't seem to matter that Charles had his long history of discovering authors and their books. Familiarity had most definitely *not* led to contempt. He was, he had to admit, in love with reading— fiction especially—and the creative mind. He had learned that some of the books he found would speak only to him.

Often, however, some he loved would become best sellers. With the best sellers, Charles felt he was sharing a delightful secret with the world. There was magic in discovering a new writer. A contagious sort of magic that had infected Robert. There was nothing that Charles enjoyed more than hearing someone recommend a book he'd published to another.

"You've found something?"

Robert shrugged, but he also handed the manuscript over a smile right on the edge of his lips and shining eyes that flicked to the manuscript over and over again. "Yes, I think so." He wasn't confident enough yet to feel certain, but Charles had noticed for some time that Robert was getting closer and closer to no longer needing anyone to guide him.

"I'll look it over soon."

It was the end of the day and Charles had a headache building behind his eyes. He always did on the days when he had to deal with the bestseller Thomas Spencer. He was too successful for his own good and expected any publishing company to bend entirely to his will.

Robert watched Charles load the manuscript into his satchel, bouncing just a little before he pulled back and cleared his throat. The boy—man, Charles supposed—smoothed his suit, flashed a grin, and left the office. Leaving for the day wasn't a bad plan. He took his satchel and—as usual—had dinner at his club before retiring to a corner of the room with an overstuffed armchair, an Old-Fashioned, and his pipe.

Charles glanced around the club, noting the other regulars. Most of them were bachelors who found it easier to eat at the club than to employ a cook. Every once in a while there was a family man who'd escaped the house for an evening with the gents, but for the most part —it was bachelors like himself.

When Charles opened the neat pages of 'Joseph Jones's *The Chronicles of Harper's Bend,* he intended to read only a small portion of the book. To get a feel for what Robert had seen and perhaps determine whether it was worth a more thorough look. After a few pages, Charles decided upon just a few more. A few more pages after that, and he left his club to return home and finish the book by his own fire.

It might have been early summer, but they were also in the middle of a ferocious storm. Charles preferred the crackle of fire wherever possible when he read, as well as a good cup of tea. There was no question that the book was well done. There was no question that Charles would be contacting the author and making an offer on the book. *The Chronicles of Harper's Bend* was, in fact, so captivating in its honesty, he couldn't quite decide whether this author loved the small towns of England or despised them. He rather felt it might be both.

Either way, it was quietly sarcastic and so true to the little village that raised Charles Aaron that he felt he might turn the page and discover the old woman who'd lived next door to his parents or the vicar of the church he'd attended as a boy. Charles felt as though he knew the people stepping off the pages.

Yes, Charles thought, yes. This one, he thought, *this* would be a best seller. Charles could feel it in his bones. He tapped out his pipe into the ashtray. This would be one of those books he looked back on with pride at having been the first to know that this book was the next big thing. Despite the lateness of the hour, Charles approached his bedroom with an energized delight. A letter would be going out in the morning.

∾

GEORGETTE MARSH

It was on the very night that Charles read the *Chronicles* that Miss Georgette Dorothy Marsh paced, once again, in front of her fireplace. The wind whipped through the town of Bard's Crook sending a flurry of leaves swirling around the graves in the small churchyard and then shooing them down to a small lane off of High Street where the elderly Mrs. Henry Parker had been awake for some time. She had woken worried over her granddaughter who was recovering too slowly from the measles.

The wind rushed through the cottages at the end of the lane, causing the gate at the Wilkes house to rattle. Dr. Wilkes and his wife were curled up together in their bed sharing warmth in the face of the changing weather. A couple much in love, snuggling into their beds on a windy evening was a joy for them both.

The leaves settled into a pile in the corner of the picket fence right at the very last cottage on that lane of Miss Georgette Dorothy Marsh.

Throughout most of Bard's Crook, people were sleeping. Their hot water bottles were at the ends of their beds, their blankets were piled high, and they went to bed prepared for another day. The unseasonable chill had more than one household enjoying a warm cup of milk at bedtime, though not Miss Marsh's economizing household.

Miss Marsh, unlike the others, was not asleep. She didn't have a fire as she was quite at the end of her income and every adjustment must be made. If she were going to be honest with herself, and she very much didn't want to be—she was past the end of her income. Her account had become overdraft, her dividends had dried up, and it might be time to recognize that her last-ditch effort of writing a book about her neighbors had not been successful.

She had looked at the lives of folks like Anthony Trollope who both worked and wrote novels and Louisa May Alcott who wrote to relieve the stress of her life and to help bring in financial help. As much as Georgette loved to read, and she did, she loved the idea that somewhere out there an author was using their art to restart their lives. There was a romance to being a writer, but she wondered just how many writers were pragmatic behind the fairytales they crafted. It wasn't, Georgette thought, going to be her story like Louisa May Alcott. Georgette was going to do something else.

"Miss Georgie," Eunice said, "I can hear you. You'll catch something dreadful if you don't sleep." The sound of muttering chased Georgie, who had little doubt Eunice was complaining about catching something dreadful herself.

"I'm sorry, Eunice," Georgie called. "I—" Georgie opened the door to her bedroom and faced the woman. She had worked for Mr. and Mrs. Marsh when Georgie had been born and in all the years of loss and change, Eunice had never left Georgie. Even now when the economies made them both uncomfortable. "Perhaps—"

"It'll be all right in the end, Miss Georgie. Now to bed with you."

Georgette did not, however, go to bed. Instead, she pulled out her pen and paper and listed all of the things she might do to further economize. They had a kitchen garden already, and it provided the vast majority of what they ate. They did their own mending and did not buy new clothes. They had one goat that they milked and made their own cheese. Though Georgette had to recognize that she rather feared goats. They were, of all creatures, devils. They would just randomly knock one over.

Georgie shivered and refused to consider further goats. Perhaps she could tutor someone? She thought about those she knew and realized that no one in Bard's Crook would hire the quiet Georgette Dorothy Marsh to influence their children. The village's wallflower and cipher? Hardly a legitimate option for any caring parent. Georgette was all too aware of what her neighbors thought of her. She rose again, pacing more quietly as she considered and rejected her options.

Georgie paced until quite late and then sat down with her pen and paper and wondered if she should try again with her writing. Something else. Something with more imagination. She had started her book with fits until she'd landed on practicing writing by describing an episode of her village. It had grown into something more, something beyond Bard's Crook with just conclusions to the lives she saw around her.

When she'd started *The Chronicles of Harper's Bend,* she had been more desperate than desirous of a career in writing. Once again, she recognized that she must do something and she wasn't well-suited to anything but writing. There were no typist jobs in Bard's Crook, no secretarial work. The time when rich men paid for companions for their wives or elderly mothers was over, and the whole of the world was struggling to survive, Georgette included.

She'd thought of going to London for work, but if she left her snug little cottage, she'd have to pay for lodging elsewhere. Georgie sighed into her palm and then went to bed. There was little else to do at that moment. Something, however, must be done.

This book is currently available.

Cinnamon Rolls & Cyanide

Tea & Temptation

Donuts & Danger

Scones & Scandal

Lemonade & Loathing

Wedding Cake & Woe

Honeymoons & Honeydew

The Pumpkin Problem

The Brightwater Bay Mysteries

(co-written with Carolyn L. Dean and Angela Blackmoore)

A Little Taste of Murder

(found in the Christmas boxset, The Three Carols of Cozy Christmas Murder)

A Tiny Dash of Death

A Sweet Spoonful of Cyanide

Manufactured by Amazon.ca
Bolton, ON